Bolan ducked as gunfire drilled the cabin window

More rounds exploded from the other side of the craft as he crawled to the port side and peered over the rail. A Tutsi soldier was standing on the deck of a Sea Ray docked two slips down. Bolan sighted on the man's torso, then pulled the trigger. The round from the .44 Magnum drilled the soldier through the ribs and punched him down and out of sight.

Bolan stood. "Come on!" he shouted, and watched as Walters and Ukewere jerked the others to their feet. "Tater, pick up the extra rifles and all the magazines you can round up!"

The Executioner hurried back to the wheel as Morrison helped Streak and the women onto the vessel while the others went after the munitions. Less than two minutes later, the two men leaped on board.

Without a word, Bolan threw the engine in reverse, backed out of the slip and started out into the lake. The Carver had barely left the marina when a Tutsi patrol boat roared into view around the peninsula, M-60s blazing.

MACK BOLAN ®

The Executioner

DON PENDLETON'S

EXECUTIONER®
THE
RESCUE RUN

A GOLD EAGLE BOOK FROM

WORLDWIDE.®

TORONTO • NEW YORK • LONDON
AMSTERDAM • PARIS • SYDNEY • HAMBURG
STOCKHOLM • ATHENS • TOKYO • MILAN
MADRID • WARSAW • BUDAPEST • AUCKLAND

First edition December 1995
ISBN 0-373-64204-0

Special thanks and acknowledgment to
Jerry VanCook for his contribution to this work.

RESCUE RUN

A man does what he must—in spite of personal
consequences, in spite of obstacles and dangers
and pressures...

> —John F. Kennedy
> *Profiles in Courage,*
> 1956

I've never deviated from the course I've set for my life,
no matter the circumstances. If I have to go down, I'll go
down fighting—and take as many of the enemy with me
as I can.

> —Mack Bolan

Dedicated to those who perished in
the Oklahoma City bombing.

PROLOGUE

No matter how funny his brain told him something was, his heart never laughed. True, it had been long enough now that he sometimes smiled. When he did, for a brief, fleeting moment, he'd almost feel happy, and he'd make a mental note to share the experience with Lois as soon as he saw her. Then he'd remember that he wouldn't be seeing Lois anymore. The smile would fade, and the loneliness and heartache would come back.

William "Dusty" Morrison grasped the edge of the thick curtain, watching as Denise LeFevre walked to center stage and pulled the microphone from its stand. The orchestra in the pit just in front of her began the opening bars of her first number, and Morrison could see that her smile was almost as bright as the sparkling sequins on her long black evening gown.

LeFevre held the mike away from her face long enough to clear her throat, then broke into the old Cole Porter song, "Love Me or Leave Me."

Morrison peered around the curtain to look at the audience. Black faces mostly. Here and there a Caucasian or an Arab. You couldn't say it was a bad house, but it wasn't the standing-room-only crowd they'd hoped for, either. He supposed that was to be expected. Things had been quiet in Rwanda for the past few months, since the Tutsi overthrew the Hutu government, quiet enough that Big Billy Rukanwe had felt it safe to organize this traveling variety show composed mostly of European celebrities. But in the last week, the military front Hutus for Majority Rule had reorganized in Uganda and Zaire and began threatening invasion.

Most Rwandans were at home this night. Both Hutus and Tutsis were trying to decide whether to flee the country or board up their windows and hope for the best. Negotiations between the two tribes were under way, and news sources gave it a fifty-fifty chance as to whether the war that had raged for centuries in Rwanda was about to begin again.

Morrison turned back to LeFevre and smiled. She sounded good tonight, seemed to be over the sore throat she'd complained about earlier in the week when they'd played Kigali.

He dropped the curtain and turned backstage, absently rubbing his chin. Too late, he remembered the makeup.

"Dusty! Dusty! Dusty!"

Morrison heard the stage whisper to his right as a hand grabbed his sleeve. He stopped, turning to see Henri Pierlot—the company's makeup artist—standing next to him. "Streak," as the cast called the little Belgian, shook the index finger on his free hand back and forth in admonishment. "Dusty, you cannot do that."

"Sorry, Streak," Morrison apologized. "Forgot again."

Streak dropped the actor's elbow. "Oh, all right. If it was anyone but *you* . . ." His voice trailed off, then he added. "Come on, I'll touch you up."

The actor followed the Belgian to the makeup chair and took a seat. Onstage, LeFevre went into her final song. As Streak redid his makeup, Morrison stared numbly at the back of the rear curtain.

Suddenly Streak was holding a mirror in front of his face. "Well?" the little makeup artist asked, seeking approval.

Seeing his face so unexpectedly sent a jolt of anxiety through Morrison. Anxiety-depression—wasn't that what the doctor had called it? Wasn't that why he'd come out of retirement to join this theater company traveling across Africa? Wasn't that why he was taking fifty milligrams of Zoloft every morning, and wasn't that why the drug wasn't doing any good?

Morrison studied his image, seeing that even the thick stage makeup couldn't cover the wrinkles anymore. Well, good. He was getting older fast, and the faster you got old, the faster you died. A year ago he remembered telling Lois he still felt like a teenager. Now he felt as if he'd been walking the planet for at least a century.

The Belgian cleared his throat in exasperation. *"Well?"*

"You're an artist, Streak," Morrison told him, standing up. "Too bad you got to work on such an old worn-out canvas."

Streak laughed. "You've still got it, Dusty, don't kid yourself."

Morrison walked slowly back to the wing, lifted the coiled lariat off the floor and checked it for snags as Denise LeFevre ended her song.

She bowed, left the state and returned amid the applause for a final bow.

Big Billy Rukanwe moved his bulky tuxedo-clad body to the microphone, sweat glistening on his bald black head.

The show's producer-director-announcer jerked a handkerchief from a pocket and mopped his forehead. The movement and the man's size made Morrison think of Louis Armstrong, which in turn made him think of the night he and Lois had sat next to old Satchmo and his wife at the Academy Awards, which sent a swell of anguish cascading through his body.

Rukanwe spoke first in Kinyarwanda, the national language of Rwanda, then in French. Morrison understood neither, but he'd read the English translation of his introduction. He knew Big Billy was hitting the high points of his long career as the last of the B Western movie stars, and putting more emphasis on his supporting roles with Robert Mitchum, Kirk Douglas and the Duke than he deserved. Like most intros, it made him sound a lot more successful and important than he'd ever been, or felt.

Then, without really knowing how he got there, Dusty Morrison was standing behind the microphone singing "Blue Prairie" and twirling his lariat into loops, double loops and figure eights. The audience started clapping as he finished the song. He dropped the rope and drew both of the stag-handled Colt .45s from the holster encircling his waist.

Mindlessly he began the gun-twirling routine he'd practiced for nearly forty years. Gasps of astonishment followed a double Open-handed Road Agent Spin. The audience applauded as he executed a faultless Border Shift and followed it with an Over the Shoulder Toss. Twirling both Colts rapidly on his trigger fingers, he jammed them back into the holsters and then drew them again.

Morrison turned away from the audience as one of the crew stepped onstage wearing a cowboy hat similar to his own white Stetson.

"Ready," Morrison said under his breath, then nodded.

The stagehand tossed a coin in the air, and the aging cowboy drew his right-hand Peacemaker, sending a load of light bird shot through the air. The shot struck the coin and sent it spinning offstage. He twirled the Colt back into his holster, nodding, and another coin sailed upward. Morrison repeated the performance with his left hand, then drew both revolvers simultaneously and shot a pair of coins.

He was about to draw again when Big Billy Rukanwe suddenly rushed onstage and grabbed the microphone. Again the Rwandan producer spoke in Kinyarwanda. This time Morrison had no translation to read and therefore no idea of Rukanwe's words. But the sudden panic of the audience as they rushed the doors told Morrison all he needed to know.

Outside the theater, he heard the first shots as Rwanda returned to war.

1

Mack Bolan, a.k.a. the Executioner, had seen the flames of the burning Petroglaz building as the Air Burundi DC-10 passed over it. The wind had been with them all the way, and he knew the air would be filled with smoke as he deplaned.

It was. The smoke smelled like oil. And mixed with the oil smell was the stench of burning human flesh.

He hurried into the terminal, his flight bag in one hand, a black leather passport case in the other. So far the bands of Hutu rebels that had begun rioting in Kigali hadn't reached the Kanombe airport, which was twelve kilometers from the center of the city. But they would. And when they did, the scant number of Tutsi government soldiers trying to protect the runways would fall to their machetes, clubs and rifles.

The warrior stopped at the end of the immigration line behind an old woman wearing traditional Hutu dress and carrying an umbrella. Ahead, he could see a thin Rwandan customs official hurriedly stamping passports and advising incoming passengers to get to their hotels quickly and stay there.

Setting his bag on the tile floor, Bolan reached under his sport coat, casually running his fingers along the cord-covered handle of the synthetic Stealth Hawk knife in his waistband. The airport metal detectors, combined with the short notice on which he'd come to Rwanda, had necessitated leaving his standard Beretta 93-R 9 mm pistol and .44 Magnum Desert Eagle behind. The high-tech plastic blade had been the only weapon he'd been able to pass through the detectors, but Hal Brognola, his contact at the U.S. Department of Justice and the director of Stony Man Farm's counterterrorist teams, had promised to forward firepower through a Rwandan contact.

Bolan didn't yet know exactly what weapons he'd be carrying in this war-ravaged nation, but something with a little more "reach" than the Stealth Hawk should be waiting for him after he cleared customs.

The customs man's stamp slapped down on a passport. Bolan pushed his bag ahead of him with his foot as the line edged forward. As he waited, his mind drifted back over what Brognola had told him only hours earlier.

"Washington's abandoned him," Brognola had said, referring to William "Dusty" Morrison, the aging Western movie actor who had been traveling with a Belgian variety stage show in Africa. "The election's less than a year away, the polls tell the President that voters are sick of our overseas involvement and the Man's determined to stay out of this. As far as the President's concerned, big guy, there *is* no Dusty Morrison. I've been given strict orders to keep you and the other Stony Man teams out of it, too."

Bolan looked up as he heard the customs man's stamp come down again with another loud bang. A tall, slender black man, close to seven feet, grabbed his passport and hurried away. The man was Tutsi—or Watusi, as they had been commonly known in the West. Within that tribe a six-footer was considered short.

The Hutus, on the other hand, were shorter and usually more broad. Members of both races were easy to pick out, which made uniforms superfluous each time war broke out in Rwanda.

Which it did with disturbing regularity. The Hutus and Tutsis had been fighting each other for more than five hundred years. Each tribe had taken its turn at government control, and each time the power shifted hands, multitudes of whichever dynasty was on the losing end were slaughtered by the victors. The underdog then organized into resistance groups—like the current Hutus for Majority Rule—and the vicious circle of death began anew.

The elderly woman with the umbrella handed her passport to the customs man and Bolan's thoughts returned to Brognola. "If you go after him, you're on your own," Brognola had said. "No communication, no backup, no help if you get caught over there."

The Executioner caught himself smiling as he remembered those words. He'd been tempted to say, "So what else is new, Hal?" but the big Fed's somber demeanor had stopped him.

"Do we have anybody we can trust over there?" Bolan had asked.

"Except for the man who'll meet you with weapons, no. Besides Bill Morrison, the show's cast is Belgian. And as you might know, the League of Nations took Rwanda from the Germans after World War I and gave it to Belgium. Brussels found it serviceable to rule through the Tutsi *mwami,* or king, until a Hutu uprising in 1959 finally chased him out." He paused and took a deep breath. "Remember that the Hutus account for almost ninety percent of Rwanda's population. They took over."

"Let me guess the rest," Bolan said. "Besides hating the Hutus, the Tutsis are still mad at the Belgians for hanging them out to dry."

"That's right. And the Hutus are angry that the Belgians installed the Tutsis to begin with."

"So either side is going to kill the Belgians if they get to them before I do," Bolan said. "But Morrison's American."

There was a long pause on Brognola's end. "It's always open season on Americans," he finally said. The G-man's tone of voice revealed that he had no doubt that Dusty Morrison would die if Bolan didn't evacuate him fast.

"This sounds like it's important to you, Hal." There had to be more to this than Brognola had told him so far. The Justice man was contemplating the direct violation of a presidential order.

"Bill Morrison and I go way back, Striker."

What it amounted to was simple: Hal Brognola and Dusty Morrison were friends. And Brognola was Bolan's friend. He and the Justice man had fought side by side over the years, facing both foreign and home-grown enemies. They'd risked their lives for each other more times than the warrior could count.

And through it all, Brognola had remained a loyal, dedicated law enforcement officer who'd never asked for a personal favor—only that his men do what was right.

Bolan's jaw set tightly as the Hutu woman ahead of him was processed, then walked away. What Brognola wanted now might border on a personal favor, but it was also the right thing to do. America couldn't abandon a citizen overseas just because it might hurt someone in an election.

Bolan stepped up to the counter.

The customs agent held up his hand. "English?" he asked.

"American," Bolan said.

The customs man nodded. "Passport," he demanded. "Visa."

The warrior opened the black leather case and pulled out the small blue booklet. He opened it to the page with his picture and handed it to the man. The yellow visa form was folded inside.

The gaunt official looked at the picture, then at Bolan. "Why you come Rwanda—" he glanced back at the passport "—Mr. John Wesley Collier?"

Bolan nodded toward the document. "Like it says I'm a journalist."

The customs man frowned.

"A reporter," Bolan explained. "Newspapers?" He held his left hand out, palm up and pantomimed a scribbling motion on top of it with his right. "A writer."

"Ah, yes," the official said. "You write about our country and all the bad things here?"

Bolan shrugged. "Whatever I see. Good or bad."

The customs man nodded. "There are both. Like all place."

The warrior grabbed his bag, shoved his passport case into his coat pocket and hurried through the terminal, thinking of his new identity as John Wesley Collier. Generally he used the aliases Rance Pollock or Mike Belasko, but this mission called for special considerations.

Any mission that violated a direct presidential order did.

Bolan let his hand run along the rail as he neared the terminal door. Rance Pollock, Mike Belasko, John Wesley Collier—it didn't make much difference to him. There was another name he had been known by ever since Vietnam, and it was that appellation, that personality really, that intended to rescue Dusty Morrison. A half dozen steps from the front door of the airport, Mack Bolan became the Executioner.

Which was a good thing. Because three steps later, three Hutu Majority Rule hardmen wearing olive-drab fatigues and black headbands burst through the door and began spraying the terminal with bullets.

The Executioner dived under a volley of 9 mm gun-fire as the men opened up. He knew who they were—he'd recognized the black headbands as soon as the gunners burst into the terminal. Majority Rule was a Hutu terrorist faction dedicated to returning the Rwandan government to their tribe, and they didn't care who died in their quest.

Screams and moans echoed around the warrior as he hit the floor on his shoulder, rolled forward and came up into a kneeling position just below the Belgian-made Vigneron subgun jumping in the hands of the man in the middle of the trio. His ears ringing with the 9 mm explosions, he drew the Stealth Hawk knife and swept the serrated edge across the inside of the terrorist's right wrist.

Bolan felt the teeth of the knife bite into tendon. The subgun quit firing, falling from the Majority Rule shooter's nearly severed hand.

The warrior caught the weapon as it fell. He stood and saw the Hutu's horrified eyes as the man stared at his severed tendon.

Twisting the gun barrel under the terrorist's chin, Bolan pulled the trigger. Four full-auto 9 mm bullets slammed into the gunner's head, driving him backward to the ground.

The Executioner shoved the knife Hawk back into the sheath inside his waistband as he stooped to sweep an extra 32-round magazine from the field vest of the corpse. Jamming it into his belt next to the synthetic knife, he turned back toward the terminal.

The other two Majority Rule hardmen had fanned out, unaware that their partner had fallen behind them. One, a burly black man with a full beard, stood twenty feet to the Executioner's left at a forty-five-degree angle, spraying a sustained burst across the large room.

The other man had leaped over the short carpet-covered wall of a ticket booth, bracing his elbows on the counter as he fired into the crowd.

Men, women and children continued to scream, diving behind chairs, ticket counters, any available cover. Those caught in the open fell to the onslaught in flurries of blood.

Bolan jammed the metal stock of the subgun against his shoulder and turned it toward the bearded Hutu. Dropping the front sight on the man's belt, he squeezed the trigger.

The subgun jumped in the Executioner's hands, climbing slightly each time the bolt worked back and forth. When he let up on the trigger, the man in the green fatigues lay dead on the concrete floor, bullet holes perforating his body from belt to armpit.

The warrior swung the weapon to his right. The terrorist behind the counter caught the movement in his peripheral vision and dropped below the barrier.

Bolan lowered the subgun and squeezed the trigger, drilling a 3-round burst into the counter. The parabellum rounds left ragged holes in the carpeting, but the whine of lead against metal, and the whir that raced back past his ear, told the Executioner that beneath the carpeting lay steel.

He had no time to curse his luck. The shooter behind the counter rose over the barrier and leveled his weapon at the Executioner's chest. Bolan dived to the floor a split second ahead of the full-auto volley that raced his way, feeling the secondary energy of the rounds as they displaced the air above his back.

Hitting the floor on his belly, the Executioner snapped another trio of rounds toward the counter, but the gunner had already dropped down again. Rolling quickly across the floor, Bolan came to rest against the counter directly across from the one where the terrorist hid. He dropped the near-empty magazine from the subgun and shoved a full load into the receiver. Kneeling at the edge of the counter corner, he trained the subgun barrel on his enemy's position.

The deadly game of cat and mouse began.

The warrior breathed steadily, monitoring each breath so he could cut it off and squeeze the trigger as soon as a target appeared again. Moments later the top of an OD boonie hat rose above the counter. Lining up the front and rear sights, his finger started back on the trigger, then suddenly stopped.

The man behind the counter had a visual disadvantage. He was blind to the Executioner's movements unless he rose over the barrier. But blind didn't mean stupid, and unless Bolan missed his guess, the rising hat was a decoy.

The hat rose to its brim, then stopped. The center of the crown seemed to jut up slightly higher than the sides, and at the very top the warrior could barely make out a small, circular protrusion.

Just about the size of the muzzle of a submachine gun.

Bolan rolled forward onto his belly, silently inching across the concrete toward the other counter. The man behind the barrier had been hoping the Executioner had retreated. He was testing the water—raising the hat on the end of his gun barrel in order to draw Bolan's fire and determine if he was still there.

The warrior made it to the counter and went flat on his back, his ear pressed to the carpet-covered metal, his subgun aimed upward. On the other side of the counter, he could hear the terrorist's nervous breathing.

Five minutes went by. Finally satisfied that his enemy was no longer there, the Majority Rule hardman rose to his feet on the other side of the carpeted steel. A moment later the terrorist vaulted the barrier, landing on his feet with his back to the Executioner.

The man had spotted Bolan below him as he jumped, and as soon as his feet hit the floor he began twisting back, his subgun seeking a target.

The terrorist was a half second too slow. Bolan had zeroed in on the shooter and pulled the trigger, unleashing a long burst that drove the man backward, dead before he hit the floor.

Sirens sounded in the distance as the Executioner got to his feet, dropped the submachine gun on the concrete and hurried out of the terminal. He joined a throng of people in a mixture of traditional tribal robes and western clothing as they hurried down the sidewalk.

As he passed the corner of the terminal building and headed toward a row of cabs and minibuses, the Executioner felt an arm suddenly wrap around his neck and jerk him back.

The odor of sweat and after-shave filled the Executioner's nostrils as he was pulled out of sight to the side of the building. Instinctively he drove an elbow backward and felt it ram into a hard set of abdominal muscles. A stifled groan met his ears.

Pivoting on the balls of his feet, the Executioner saw a Caucasian man in his late fifties bent double, struggling for air. Around five feet eight inches and a well-preserved one-eighty pounds, the man wore a shaggy white mustache, blue jeans, a plain white T-shirt and black athletic shoes.

Bolan drew the Stealth Hawk knife and pressed the serrated edge into the man's throat as he backed him against the side of the building. As the man caught his breath, the warrior used his free hand to pat him down.

He found a blue-worn Government Model .45 automatic behind the man's right kidney and an identical weapon on the man's left.

Shoving one of the .45s into his belt, Bolan stuck the other under the man's chin. "Any other tricks up your sleeve?" he asked.

The white-haired man looked up, shook his head and grinned.

The Executioner frowned. A smile was hardly the expression he'd expected from a man who'd been disarmed while trying to kill him. "Want to tell me who sent you and what you want?'' he said. "Or should I just pull the trigger right now?''

The older man's grin widened as the color came back to his face and his breathing returned to normal. "Brognola sent me. Hal told me you were a hard case. But I just had to find out for myself.''

EXOTIC BIRDS CHIRPED and chimpanzees chattered in the overhead tree branches as the five men and one woman made their way through Rwanda's Rugege Forest.

Bringing up the rear of the procession, Dusty Morrison glanced over his shoulder, looking for anyone— Hutu or Tutsi—who might be following. The only thing the two tribes seemed to have in common was their mutual hatred for Belgians, and the Hutus who'd stormed the theater had proved that hatred by hacking up the cast members with their machetes. Besides Big Billy and his chauffeur, Mwinyi, only Dusty Morrison, Denise LeFevre, Hubert Spaak and Streak had escaped.

The Western star's stomach recoiled at the memory of the blood that had flowed. The surviving Belgians had been lucky, and so had he. He didn't know how the Hutus felt about Americans, but he knew they sure hadn't taken time out of their crazed murder spree to check anybody's passport.

Turning back to the front, Morrison watched Streak walking along. The makeup artist sniffled softly with every step, and as he reached a low branch he pushed it forward, then let go.

The leaf-covered bough snapped back toward Morrison's eyes, and just in time he reached up and caught it. With another quick glance to his rear, he ducked under the limb and plodded on. What if he *did* catch a glimpse of somebody following them? he wondered. What would he do? He'd had a fistfight or two in his younger days and always come out okay, but he'd never been in a real life-or-death struggle. True, he'd pulled the trigger of both Colts as they left the theater, firing bird shot at a pair of crazed Hutus with machetes. But the light loads had done little more than slow the men down while Denise and Spaak jumped into Big Billy's limousine.

A smile spread slowly across the aging actor's face. So, what would he do if it came to a fight? He'd fight. Why not? If he won, he'd live. If he didn't, he'd die and be with Lois. He had no downside on this one, and for a second he wondered just which victory he'd really prefer.

The procession started down an embankment, and Morrison could see Big Billy Rukanwe at the front of the line. Mwinyi walked next to the overweight producer, and behind them Hubert Spaak had taken Denise LeFevre by the elbow and was helping her along. Denise still wore her gown from the show. Practically in shreds now, it made her look like she was playing Jane in a Tarzan movie.

Morrison paused before starting down the embankment, running the back of his sleeve across his eyebrows to mop up the sweat. They'd had no time to change before fleeing the theater, and he supposed he should thank God that his costume was boots, jeans, chaps and hat. He'd fared much better on this hike than Spaak, who performed in a tuxedo.

Digging his boot heels into the soft vine-covered ground, Morrison started down the slope sideways. At the bottom Streak had fallen to his hands and knees. The little makeup man was openly crying now, tears rolling down his cheeks to mat the wispy light brown goatee that covered his chin.

Morrison leaned down and grasped the man's arm. "Come on, pardner," he whispered. "Can't be too much farther now." He helped Streak to his feet and pushed him gently up the other side of the embankment.

Rukanwe had stopped next to a tree stump at the edge of a clearing. The rest of the cast members gathered around as he placed his feet side by side, then carefully paced seven steps past the tree line. Mwinyi unfolded the collapsible entrenching tool he'd been carrying and began to dig.

Morrison wiped the sweat from his brow again and looked around as he waited. He wasn't sure where they were, just that they had driven from Cyangugu to the edge of the Rugege Forest, hidden the limo on an out-of-the-way trail, then taken off through the trees on foot.

When screech of steel on steel broke the stillness in the forest, Morrison turned his attention back to the digging. Mwinyi's entrenching tool had uncovered a door hidden a foot or so below the surface, and now he used the tool to scrape the dirt from the edges before reaching down for the handle.

Slowly, creaking from lack of oil, the door opened.

Morrison was the last one to step onto the staircase, which led to a landing fifteen feet below. Rukanwe stood at an open door, ushering the cast members out of sight into the fortress.

The aging actor closed the door above his head, then turned to see that Rukanwe had followed the others into the house and out of sight. His hand on the railing, he slowly walked down the steps to the landing, recalling the radio reports they'd listened to in French as the limo fled the city of Cyangugu. Streak had translated for his benefit, and he'd learned that what had gone on outside the theater hadn't been an isolated incident.

All over Rwanda, the nation was once again in chaos as the Hutus and Tutsi fought for power. Men, women and children were being shot, speared and hacked to death with machetes. The Tutsi government militia was killing Hutus. The Hutu rebels were slaughtering Tutsis. And both tribes were butchering any stray Belgians they found in revenge for the sins of the Belgians' fathers.

Reaching the bottom of the stairs, Morrison stepped through the door into a large living room. He heard voices coming from elsewhere in the subterranean house, and took in the living room as he walked toward them. Rukanwe had prepared well. The furnishings were livable, if not elegant. Two couches and several easy chairs faced a combination television set-

VCR against the front wall. Bookcases lined the rest of the walls, with the shelves around the TV reserved for videocassette tapes. A six-chair dining table stood at the rear of the living room.

The aging actor followed the sound of voices through a kitchen that led to another hallway. He passed the open door to a vacant bedroom and found the others in a similar room at the end of the hall.

LeFevre, Spaak and Streak were seated on the bed facing Rukanwe and Mwinyi, who stood in front of a chest of drawers. Big Billy was speaking in French.

"I had it built years ago," Rukanwe said, switching to English when he saw Morrison slip into the room. "I have come here before, when no place else in Rwanda was safe."

Spaak looked him in the eye. "Both tribes are hunting down Belgians," he said. "*We're* Belgians." He glanced quickly at Morrison as the man took a place against the wall. "At least most of us. And they know we're in the country—especially *me.*"

The producer didn't answer.

"When can we get out of the country?" LeFevre asked.

Rukanwe shrugged. "As soon as things die down."

"When will that be?" Spaak demanded. He looked around the room. "This isn't my idea of a green-room, Billy. My garage is decorated better than this place. It's a prison. An underground dungeon."

"It is a sanctuary," Rukanwe said, and a quick grimace of hurt passed over his face.

Morrison felt a jolt of anger lance through him. Big Billy Rukanwe had risked his life bringing them here. Spaak's ingratitude was detestable, though not surprising to anyone who knew the man.

The aging actor had known both Spaak and Rukanwe for only a few days, but understood them both well. While he might be a little weak in the decision-making department, Rukanwe was a friendly man and treated them well. The fact that he hung out with gangster types like Zaid Karsimbi hadn't gone unnoticed by Morrison, but he chalked that up to show business. Plenty of Hollywood's finest did the same.

Hubert Spaak, on the other hand, had proved to be a selfish, shallow, spoiled little brat. He was in his midtwenties, and European stardom had been dropped in his lap. Before he'd known what was happening, he was making movies with America's leading ladies. Spaak was too immature to recognize his good fortune as the luck of the draw rather than talent. He had decided he was God's gift to the fans— particularly the female fans—and that life not only owed him a living, but a luxurious one at that. He might be Belgian by birth, but he lived in Bel Air now, and acted more Ugly American than any native-born Yank Dusty Morrison had ever met.

The older man watched Spaak try to drape an arm around Denise LeFevre's shoulders as he continued to stare hatefully at the man who'd saved his life. The woman gently shrugged it off.

Morrison had to grin. Ever since the show had opened, he'd watched the shock in Spaak's eyes each time the middle-aged beauty rebuffed his overtures. Spaak couldn't believe she didn't go for him like all the starlets he'd worked with, and LeFevre's conquest was becoming an obsession with him.

"Does anyone have any questions before I go?" Rukanwe asked.

"You aren't staying?" LeFevre said anxiously.

Rukanwe shook his head. "I must return to Kigali. My wife has taken our daughter to her sister's house, but who knows if that is safe? We may all return. If not, I have another place where we can hide until things have settled down again."

A spark of fear flickered in Spaak's eyes, and Morrison couldn't help the satisfaction it gave him to see it. "You ought to stay," Spaak said. "You said you built this place for emergencies. If this isn't an emergency, I don't know what is."

Rukanwe chuckled, and it was obvious he took a certain perverse delight in the young elitist's discomfort, too. "Stay in Rwanda long enough," he said, "and you will learn that there are emergencies . . . and there are *emergencies.*"

Spaak glared at him with a mixture of fright and anger.

The Rwandan turned back to the group as a whole. "You will find food in the pantries. There are two bedrooms, and a full kitchen, but I regret only one bath."

"Oh, terrific," Spaak said under his breath.

"There are many books and movies." Rukanwe glanced at Spaak. "We even have *Fire Run,* and some of your others, Hubert." He paused, then added, "I hope you will all be as comfortable as possible."

"Books, videotapes and a bathroom," Spaak practically spit out. "Yeah, we'll be about as comfortable as we would be at a cheap motel."

Rukanwe sighed and turned to Morrison. "Do you have any questions before I leave, Dusty?" he asked.

The actor nodded. "The topside door. It's gonna be obvious it was just dug up."

Rukanwe smiled. "We will put the dirt back, then build a small fire over it. When it burns out, the ashes will make it look as if campers stayed here overnight."

"Good. Is there any way for us to see what's going on above the ground?" He couldn't help but think a man resourceful enough to build this place would have thought of that, as well.

The producer slapped his forehead. "I am so sorry. I almost forgot. Please follow me." He turned and walked out of the room and down the hall, Morrison and the others at his heels. Stopping in front of a door, he opened it to reveal a water heater and air-conditioning unit. A long, narrow pipe stopped at eye level, the other end disappearing into the ceiling.

Morrison stepped forward and saw that the eye-level end of the pipe had been cut at an angle. A small mirror was fastened to the inside, and when he looked into it, he could see green leaves in the mirror at the top of the homemade periscope. He turned back to Rukanwe. "One more thing," he said.

The Rwandan raised his eyebrows.

"What do we do if they *do* find this place?"

Rukanwe's face told Dusty the producer didn't know.

The cast followed Rukanwe and Mwinyi through the living room to the stairs and watched the two men exit the underground house. Morrison stayed at the top of the steps, listening until he could hear the faint crackling of burning wood.

When he returned to the living room, LeFevre and Spaak sat on the couch, staring at the television. He turned toward the screen and saw Spaak racing through a burning building with a beautiful blonde on one arm, a submachine gun in the other. "See that overhead beam?" Spaak was telling Denise LeFevre excitedly. "Watch it fall...okay...*there!* That was it. It missed me by maybe two inches!"

Morrison walked to the bookshelf, pulled down the first book he saw and opened it. His eyes fixed on the page, but didn't read. Behind him, he heard Spaak talking again about the dangers he'd faced while shooting *Fire Run*. He turned toward them as LeFevre rose and started toward the kitchen. Spaak continued to stare at the screen, now watching himself as he shoved the blonde into a car and dived in after her.

Hubert Spaak made a great action-movie hero, Morrison had to admit. He looked the part, with his bulging muscles and tough-guy profile. But what was happening to them now wasn't a movie. The bullets they'd already faced, and might well face again, weren't blanks.

As he settled into an armchair with his book, the aging actor wondered how Hubert Spaak would react to violence if there was no director around to yell "Cut!"

2

"Just exactly who are you?" Bolan asked as he opened the passenger door of the rusty gold Ford LTD. The Executioner didn't yet know how big a part Brognola had assigned the older man, or whether he could be trusted.

The white-haired man slid behind the wheel, stuck the key in the ignition and fired up the engine. "Walter Walters," he said. "Everybody calls me Tater, though."

"Why?"

Walters chuckled. "The Tater part came in Nam," he replied, "'cause of my Southern accent and the fact that whenever we took R & R in Thailand I went looking for the nearest place that served French fries." He threw the car into drive. "The Walter part, well, it seemed as good as any other name. So I just used it twice."

"That's not your real name, then."

Tater Walters's chest vibrated with humor again. "Nope. Can't remember the real one. Lost my memory 'bout the time I joined the French foreign legion after Nam." He pulled the LTD away from the curb.

"Then again, I'm guessin' your mama didn't stick you with no moniker like John Wesley Collier, neither."

"No." What Walter "Tater" Walters was really telling him was that his real name was wanted somewhere. Many soldiers in that position chose the French foreign legion, where they could get a fresh start with no questions asked.

The fact that he was wanted didn't automatically mean Tater Walters couldn't be trusted. But it didn't mean he could be, either. But if Brognola trusted him—and the Justice man did or he wouldn't have given him the name Bolan was using in Rwanda—that was good enough for the Executioner.

Bolan turned toward the man behind the wheel. "How is it you know Brognola?"

Walters guided the LTD away from the airport and started the twelve-kilometer drive into Kigali. He frowned. "I got me a little cottage-industry business over here," he finally said. "Sell information to the Feds at home. Pretty simple thing, really. Got my contacts, and I keep my eyes and ears open. Then when the DEA or FBI or CIA calls, or your buddy Brognola needs to know something, they ask me. If I don't already know the answer, I usually know how to go about getting it."

The LTD continued to rattle down the smoke-filled road, passing groups of people fleeing the riots in the city. Bolan watched their faces. They didn't look particularly excited. Their expressions indicated they'd resigned themselves to the periodic violence that erupted in Rwanda—and were too bone weary to care anymore.

"And I do favors for a price, as well," Walters continued as they reached the city limits. "Like coming up with guns for people when they need them."

"Mercenary?" Bolan asked.

Walters turned to face the Executioner, his face turning serious. "I suppose so. But get this straight. I only work for the good guys."

Bolan nodded. He felt the twin Government Model .45s digging into his flesh on both his sides. "These 1911s for me?" he asked.

"Hell no," Walters said. "Those are *my* babies. We're on our way to get your stuff. But now that you mention it—" he stretched a hand across the seat "—I'll take them back now."

Bolan jerked one of the well-worn .45 automatics from his belt and handed it to the man. "I'll keep the other until we pick up my weapons," he said. "Where are they?"

Walters returned the .45 to his belt. "I stashed them in a vacant house. Brognola said you wanted a .44 Magnum Desert Eagle and a Beretta 93-R."

Bolan nodded.

Walters chuckled. "Well, people in hell want ice water, too. This is Rwanda, I'm afraid. I got you the best I could."

The Executioner understood. "What?" he asked.

"Smith & Wesson Model 629 for the .44 Magnum, and your 9 mm pistol's gonna have to be a Browning.

I came up with extra mags for the Hi-Power and speed-loaders for the wheel gun.''

Bolan nodded. Both were fine guns. The .44 Magnum revolver would provide the same explosive power and penetration as the Desert Eagle, even if it fell a few rounds short in firepower.

The LTD turned onto Avenue Paul VI and cruised past the Kigali military camp. The rioting had moved away from the center of town as the Tutsi-controlled army organized and began to patrol the street. Men in jeeps and personnel carriers, as well as foot soldiers, stared at the Ford as they passed. Finally one of the vehicles pulled up alongside, and someone waved them to the curb.

"Pain in the ass dogfaces," Walters muttered. Bolan watched him reach into his back pocket and pull out a billfold. As two soldiers wearing jungle-camouflage fatigues dropped down from the jeep behind them, he took out several Rwandan franc notes, then replaced the wallet. "They don't cost much, but they're a damned nuisance," he complained.

The soldiers split at the rear of the car and came to the windows, both shoving the barrels of Belgian FN FAL assault rifles into the vehicle. The man on Walters's side said something in Kinyarwanda, and the mercenary answered, handing him the money.

A brief argument ensued, then Walters turned to Bolan. "Son of a bitch is in a difficult mood," he said. "Wants American. You got any greenbacks on you?"

Bolan reached into his pocket and pulled out two twenties. He handed one to Walters and stuck the other out his window.

The soldier on his side gasped. A moment later, the two men walked back to their jeep, conversing excitedly.

"That's just about ten times more than they expected," Walters said. "It makes us look like rich Americans, so let's get out of here before they decide to come back and rob and kill us."

Bolan noticed a ten-year-old Chevy van behind them as the LTD accelerated. Avenue Paul VI curved to the north as they circled the military camp, then angled onto Rue Député Kayuku. A glance in the passenger's sideview mirror told the Executioner the van had followed.

Walters caught his look. "Tail?" he asked.

"Maybe."

The merc guided them through a confusing series of side streets into a rundown residential area. The van kept its distance, but continued to follow.

"It's that house on the corner," Walters said, indicating a dilapidated structure with his head. He looked up at the mirror. "They still with us?"

"Yeah." Bolan's gaze flickered to a tall, slender black man who stood on the porch of a clapboard house next to the one Walters had pointed out. Another tall man stood in front of a parked Datsun directly across the street. The vehicle's hood was open, the man's hands busy with the engine.

Two more suspicious characters sat in a Ford Explorer halfway down the next block.

"You catch all of them?" Bolan asked.

Walters nodded. "One on the porch, another in front of the Datsun. Two in the Explorer." He didn't have to be told not to stop, and drove down the block.

"Take us up about a half mile, then find the nearest wide spot in the road and cut a fast U," Bolan directed him. He fastened his seat belt, then flipped the safety off the Government Model pistol and pulled the slide back partway to check the chamber. Satisfied, he returned the weapon to the cocked-and-locked position and rested it in his lap.

The LTD slowed as it reached the next intersection, then suddenly Walters stomped the brakes, sending the vehicle into a 180-degree skid. He twisted the wheel violently as the tires squealed and smoked, and a second later they were speeding back toward the van in the opposite direction. "Ain't played chicken since I was a teenager," Walters said with a grin as he leaned on the accelerator.

Bolan gripped the .45 in his right hand, his left on the seat-belt buckle as the LTD raced toward the oncoming vehicle a half block away. The faces of two surprised and frightened men appeared through the van's windshield as the LTD suddenly bore down on them. The driver tried to swerve but got only halfway across the narrow street when the LTD rammed his side.

Metal crunched and glass burst as the Executioner flew forward against the seat belt. The LTD was still rocking back and forth as he flipped the seat-belt buckle's release, then bolted out of the vehicle. Walters was only a half step behind as the warrior raced toward the van and ripped open the driver's-side door.

Both of the men in the van had slammed into the windshield and been knocked unconscious. Bolan reached up, pressing an index finger into the driver's carotid artery. The pulse was still strong.

Across the van, Walters tore open the passenger door and checked the other man's throat. He glanced at Bolan and shook his head.

"Let's get this guy out of here," the Executioner said, pulling the driver's feet out of the car. Walters circled the van and grabbed the man under the arms. Together they carried him quickly to the Ford and tossed him into the backseat. Bolan got in back next to the prisoner as Walters resumed his place at the wheel.

Less than thirty seconds after the crash the LTD was chugging along the road again.

"Where you want to take him?" Walters asked.

The warrior shook his head. "It doesn't matter. Just get us out of this neighborhood and keep driving." He looked at the blood oozing from the man's forehead. "You got a first-aid kit?"

"Don't know. Maybe." Walters leaned over and dug through the glove box. "Nothing in here...hey, wait." Pulling out two red oil rags, he handed them over the seat.

As the LTD started down the street, the Executioner applied direct pressure to the man's head wound with one rag, then tied the other around his head to hold the makeshift bandage in place.

Bolan studied the unconscious man. He was tall and slender like the others they'd seen watching the house. They were dealing with the Tutsi-controlled government here, rather than the Hutu resistance.

The Executioner slapped the man lightly on the cheek and glanced up at Walters's reflection in the rearview mirror. "Find some place to park," he said. "Your car sounds like it's about to fall apart. Sorry. Maybe Brognola can foot the bill for you."

Walters turned and the Executioner saw the white-haired man's now-familiar grin. "Don't worry about it," he said. "It's not my car. I stole this piece of junk just before I picked you up."

THE EXECUTIONER GLANCED through the window as Walters pulled the LTD to a halt next to the curb. They were just off Kigali's market section in an open area of scattered houses and buildings.

The man next to him in the backseat had a narrow black face and rangy shoulders under a green T-shirt now stained black with dried blood. He opened his eyes as Bolan turned back to him.

"Who are you?" the Executioner demanded in French.

The man blinked but didn't respond.

Bolan shoved the .45 under his chin. "Who are you?" he repeated. "And don't act like you don't speak French. If you do, I'll just have my partner interrogate you in Kinyarwanda." He let it sink in, then said, "You're Tutsi, but Tutsi what?"

The man's eyes opened wide in fear, and Bolan could tell he thought the wrong answer would bring instantaneous death. But the Executioner's white skin confused him. After several seconds, he closed his eyes tight and said, "Police. Secret police."

"Why were you following us, and how'd you know about the house?"

The man opened his eyes again, surprised to still be alive. "The Twa," he said. "He said there were weapons there."

"Who's he talking about?" Bolan demanded.

"Salewe Ukewere," Walters said from the front seat. "Local con man who sells information like me. But he plays both sides of the fence."

"How'd he know about the house?" Bolan asked, jamming the gun tighter into the man's throat.

"I do not know. I swear I do not know! He told us only that there were guns stashed in the house. And since we knew they were not ours, we thought they belonged to the Hutus."

"How'd you know to follow this guy then?" Bolan asked, hooking a thumb toward Walters.

Again, the mercenary answered the question. "It's not all that unusual. I catch Ukewere tailing me every once in a while to find out what I know. He must have seen me go into the house."

"It is true!" the captive cried, looking past Bolan to the front seat. "He knew you had put guns in the house and suspected they were for the Hutu rebels. That's why he came to us!''

Bolan glanced over his shoulder.

Walters shrugged, then nodded the fact that it was likely to be true.

Bolan turned back to the bleeding man, trying to decide just how much time he should put into getting the specific weapons Walters had obtained for him. In a war-torn country like Rwanda, there were plenty of firearms available off the streets. But they wouldn't be .44 Magnums.

The Executioner jabbed his captive's neck with the .45 again. ''Where are the guns now?'' he demanded

''I do not know. In one of the surveillance vehicles, I assume.''

Bolan stared into the Tutsi's eyes, then reached across him and opened the door. ''Get out,'' he ordered.

''You are not going to kill me?''

''Not if you hurry.''

The man did.

The warrior followed him out the door and got into the front seat. Walters turned the car around and they headed back toward the residential neighborhood.

''I spotted four men,'' the Executioner said. ''Two in the surveillance car, one in front of the house and the guy fixing his engine. You see anybody else?''

Walters shook his head.

''Park out of sight a couple of blocks away,'' Bolan directed him. ''It'll be easier to take them out on foot.''

Ten minutes later Walters pulled the LTD to the curb on a side street. Bolan opened the door and got out. Staring between the houses, he could see the corner of the vacant house the next block over. "Cut through the yard there," he told Walters, pointing to the left. "You take out the guy under the Datsun's hood."

"You planning to do the rest?" Walters asked.

Bolan nodded. "Try to take him quietly. I'll wait for you."

The man in front of the Datsun needed neutralizing, but the situation also provided Bolan with an opportunity to test Tater Walters. The merc had mentioned that he'd been in Vietnam and had served in the French foreign legion, and in spite of his age, he still had the bearing of a warrior.

But Bolan had known him less than an hour. The white-haired man could be lying, and the Executioner needed to be sure he could still cut it.

He could use someone watching his back while he was in Rwanda, provided Walters had what it took.

What the warrior was doing didn't pass by the white-haired man. "A test, huh? Five'll get you ten I pass."

Bolan split from the former legionnaire as they crossed the street, cutting between two ramshackle dwellings into the backyard of the one to his right. He moved swiftly, fully aware that in his sport coat, slacks and white skin he'd look drastically out of place to anyone watching. Coming to a broken-down knee-high fence, he stepped over it into the alley, then crossed to the yard of the house that had the two men sitting out front in the Ford Explorer.

The Executioner moved along the side of the building. Peering around the front corner, he saw the two men were still in the front seat. The Explorer faced away from the vacant house where Walters had stashed the guns, but their eyes were fixed to the vehicle's sideview mirrors.

Sticking his head out slightly farther, Bolan could see across the street. The Tutsi on the porch continued to stand where he'd been with the erect posture of a soldier.

Bolan dropped to a squat and looked down the street. The man in front of the Datsun still tinkered with the engine. As he watched, Walters stepped into sight from between two houses and walked casually to the street before turning toward the Datsun. The merc held a key ring in his hand and strolled along as if walking to his car. He glanced over his shoulder briefly as he neared the Datsun, then his gaze swept up the street on both sides.

The man under the hood started to look up as the merc drew alongside the vehicle. Without breaking stride Walters reached up, grasped the hood and slammed it down on the quarry's head.

Bolan drew the .45. His eyes skimmed a triangle from the Datsun to the porch across the street and back to the Explorer. None of the other men had noticed what had happened.

The Executioner turned back to Walters. The white-haired man had opened the hood. The man whose head had been caught inside looked groggy but was still conscious. The former legionnaire shot an uppercut under the Tutsi's chin, then moved behind him, reaching up to wrap both arms around the slender neck and jerk it down.

Walters held the chokehold until the man slumped to the ground.

Bolan turned back to the house across the street, just in time to realize that they'd been made. The man on the porch was clawing at his hip holster, frantically trying to free his weapon. Too late. The warrior's Government Model pistol exploded, and the man on the porch collapsed into a heap.

The Executioner sighted the weapon on the Explorer, drilling a round into the passenger's temple, then sprinted into the street. He rounded front of the vehicle as the driver jumped out wielding a small semiautomatic pistol.

A double tap of .45 hardball rounds cut through the man's frayed white shirt and dropped him to the street.

Bolan hurried forward, picking up the weapon that had fallen from the man's hand—a Hungarian FEG .380 copy of the Walther PPK. Dropping it in the side pocket of his jacket, he saw Walters open the door of the Datsun and start rummaging inside.

The warrior opened the door of the Explorer and jerked the passenger out onto the street. Quickly he searched the front and back seats, coming up with another FEG pistol, but nothing else.

The Executioner heard a whistle and stuck his head back out of the Explorer. Down the street, he could see

Walters holding a large leather satchel in one hand. In the other hand he gripped a short black man by the scruff of the neck.

By the time Bolan reached the Datsun, sirens were sounding in the distance, and curious heads were starting to peek out of doors up and down the street. The Executioner glanced both ways. "Let's get out of here," he said, fishing through the pants of the man Walters had choked until he found the car keys. He slid behind the wheel as the white-haired mercenary shoved his struggling captive into the car and climbed in after him.

"Well, did I pass the test?" Walters asked.

Bolan twisted the key in the ignition and nodded. "That one," he said. "There's another coming up."

Even as the words left his mouth, two military jeeps rounded the corner behind them. Both jeeps held four men in OD green fatigues, and the barrels of eight assault rifles were pointed their way.

The Executioner floored the accelerator and twisted the steering wheel, angling the Datsun away from the curb. The car coughed and jerked, then moved sluggishly forward. Looking back to the mirror, he saw that the jeeps were less than a block behind them.

In the back seat, Walters had read their predicament as well as the Executioner. "We'll never outrun them," he commented.

"See if you can take out a tire," Bolan yelled over the noise as the Datsun slowly gained speed.

Walters started to open the satchel, but as he did his captive turned and reached for the door on his side.

The merc reached across the back seat, grabbed the man's arm and jerked it back. "Stay put," he ordered.

A voice speaking in Kinyarwanda came over a loudspeaker, shouting orders to the Datsun's occupants.

Opening the satchel, Walters pulled out a large stainless-steel revolver, thumbed the latch and swung out the cylinder.

Bolan watched in the mirror as Walters dumped the hollowpoint rounds back into the case and grabbed a speed-loader with his other hand. "Armor piercing," the older man shouted above the Datsun's listless engine and the roar of the oncoming jeeps.

Static crackled over the loudspeaker, then the gruff voice spoke again. Bolan didn't slow. The voice switched to French, ordering them to stop.

"No, thanks," Walters said to himself as he twisted in the seat and leaned out the open window.

The Executioner continued to try to will extra power out of the Datsun as he watched Walters in the side mirror. The older man steadied his elbows on the windowsill, then double-actioned a quick .44 Magnum slug at the lead jeep.

The round exploded behind the Executioner's ear. The bullet missed the left front tire by a foot, sending sparks shimmying down the pavement in its wake.

The Tutsi soldiers took the shot as an invitation to open up.

Dozens of rounds suddenly exploded from the assault rifles in the jeeps, taking out the back windshield of the Datsun and leaving holes in the trunk. Miraculously the rounds missed the three men in the vehicle, and the tires and other vital parts of the Datsun remained intact.

"You'd better get a tire, and you'd better get it quick," Bolan yelled, turning a corner at breakneck speed. He watched Walters take a deep breath, then lean out the window again.

This time the armor-piercing .44 Magnum round flew true, striking the left front tire and sending the lead jeep careening across the street and up into the yard of a rundown residence. Three of the soldiers bailed out a second before the vehicle crashed into the concrete steps that led to the porch. The driver was thrown out of the jeep and slammed up against the house.

The second jeep continued pursuit, with more rounds exploding into the Datsun. The front windshield went the way of the rear, and now steam began to rise from under the hood.

Walters leaned out the window again, snapping another round back toward the soldiers. The projectile missed the jeep, but the driver slowed momentarily and the men with the rifles ducked.

It was the reaction Walters had hoped for, and his next double-actioned round struck rubber. The jeep fishtailed wildly before grinding to a halt in the center of the street.

The steam from under the Datsun's hood was rising faster. Bolan turned another corner and found himself back on Rue Député Kayuku. He followed it back to Paul VI, took a left, then cut over to Rue de Nyarugungu. They were a block from Revolution Boulevard when the Datsun finally gave up the ghost, chugging to a halt as the Executioner pulled to the side of the street.

Turning, Bolan saw that the African was still unconscious from a blow Walters had administered when the man had tried to leap out of the vehicle during the gun battle. "Get him awake, stick a gun in his ribs and tell him if he makes a sound he's dead."

Walters nodded. "Sounds simple enough. You going somewhere?"

Bolan turned to look up the street. A tall structure bearing a sign that proclaimed it to be a hotel stood a block and a half away. "We need a place to lie low, regroup and find out if this guy knows anything about the actors." He cleared his throat. "I take it this is the man you were talking about?"

Walters nodded. "Salewe Ukewere. The one and only."

Bolan indicated the hotel with his head. "You know the Diplomat?"

"Upscale," Walters said. "At least for Rwanda. Might want to straighten the knot in your tie before you go in." He glanced to Ukewere. "There's a side door on the first floor that leads to the alley. Locked, but it opens from the inside."

"I'll meet you there in ten minutes," Bolan said. "Keep a low profile." He got out of the car and hurried up the street.

Though the rioting had quieted, few people were venturing out of the stores and other businesses along Revolution Boulevard. Bolan passed a dead body between two buildings, but saw no one else until he'd entered the lobby, where a reed-thin man wearing a blue blazer stood behind the desk.

The desk clerk looked up warily, his hand moving under the counter as the Executioner approached. "Any vacancies?" Bolan asked in French.

"You may take your pick," he replied, his hand coming back into view.

"One night," the warrior said, then dropped several Rwandan franc bills on the counter. He took the key to room 212 from the man, then stepped into the nearby elevator.

When the doors opened on the second floor, Bolan found a back staircase and returned to ground level. A short hunt up and down the vacant halls found the steel door to the alley, and when he opened it Walters and Ukewere were waiting.

The blow the mercenary had dealt out earlier had left Ukewere's jaw swollen and ugly. The little man's attitude was the same. He ripped off a long stream of what the Executioner suspected were Kinyarwanda curses, until Walters jammed a .45 into the man's ribs and ordered him to be quiet.

Bolan led them back up the stairs and down the hall to the door marked 212. Inside, they found a dusty room in need of paint. But Tater Walters had been right. Given what the Executioner had seen of Rwanda, the place was heaven.

Walters shoved Ukewere into a chair by the bed and took a seat on the tattered bedspread. Bolan pulled the chair from under a dressing table, turned it to face them and sat. He stared at their captive. The little man sat straight in his chair, his feet dangling a foot from the floor. A gaudy-print square-tailed sport shirt fell over his paunchy torso outside his gray slacks, and a row of cigars protruded from the shirt pocket.

"You speak English?" Bolan asked.

He got no reply.

"He does," Walters stated.

The Executioner nodded. "Your name's Ukewere?"

The African remained silent, his eyes boring hate-filled holes through the Executioner.

"This can be easy, or it can be hard," Bolan said.

Again he got no response.

The Executioner sighed and turned to Walters. "Give me the Smith."

The mercenary opened the satchel and pulled out the revolver.

Bolan snapped open the weapon, dumped the pointed armor-piercing rounds out into his hand, then stuck one back into the cylinder. Spinning the wheel, he closed it quickly again and held his hand over the space between the cylinder and the frame. "What's your name?" he repeated.

When Ukewere didn't answer, Bolan shoved the gun under his chin. Below the man's line of sight, the hand covering the cylinder moved slightly until his finger could feel the chamber that would revolve and fire when he pulled the trigger. Empty.

Bolan double-actioned the revolver and the hammer fell on the empty chamber with a loud metallic snap.

The Executioner studied Ukewere's face. It didn't change.

"The odds were pretty good on that one," Bolan said. "But they'll get worse each time we play this game." He paused. "Now what's your name?"

If anything, the defiance in Ukewere's eyes intensified.

Bolan shrugged, his left hand ensuring that the next chamber was empty, as well. "Have it your way," he said, and pulled the trigger again. The revolver snapped.

The Executioner had watched Ukewere's eyes carefully as he pulled the trigger. The man seemed devoid of fear. He either didn't care if he lived or died, or he was one fine actor under pressure.

Tracing his finger along the frame, the Executioner found the third chamber empty, too. "What's your name?" he asked, and pulled the trigger almost immediately.

Ukewere looked at the revolver, then spit on it.

Bolan sat on the bed and used the pillow to wipe off the revolver. The movement afforded him an opportunity to surreptitiously glance down to see that the next chamber was empty, but the one after that held the giant .44 Magnum round.

The Executioner stood, moved to Ukewere's side and pressed the barrel against the man's temple. "You ready to talk yet?" he asked.

No answer. As the African stared straight ahead, Bolan pulled the trigger.

Ukewere turned to look him in the eye. "Save yourself some time. Fill the gun and pull the trigger. I will never talk to you under these conditions."

Walters moved up to sit directly in front of him. "Ukewere, you are one crazy little runt, you know that?" he said. "This man's going to kill you."

"Oh, wouldn't that be terrible!" he said sarcastically. "To be dead! To lose all that I have in this Garden of Eden they call Rwanda!"

He turned back to Bolan. "Do it and get it over with," he said through gritted teeth. "You'll be doing me a favor."

Bolan studied him. The man wasn't kidding. He was ready to die.

Walters stood, exasperated. "What the hell's wrong with you, Sal?" he said. "You've played both sides of the fence all your life. You've sold information to the Hutus. Then you've turned right back around and sold the fact that the Hutus had it to the Tutsis. What's stopping you now?"

"No one has offered to pay me yet," Ukewere said calmly.

"We'll pay you with your life," Walters growled.

"My life is worth nothing. Money is."

Bolan sat on the bed next to Walters, broke open the revolver, dumped the armor-piercing round and filled the chamber with hollowpoints. He was beginning to understand Ukewere, and while the little man's attitude might make no sense on the surface, anyone who knew Rwandan history could figure it out.

The Twa Pygmies had been the original inhabitants of the region that would come to be known as Rwanda, being chased out around 1000 A.D. by the invading Tutsi. Some had remained and become part of the new society, but always as second-class citizens. Rwandans as a whole had little chance of forging a decent life for themselves, and prejudice from both Tutsi and Hutu made it even worse for the Twa. The Executioner suspected that racial bigotry accounted to a high degree for Ukewere's development as a con man who had so little regard for the lives of others—or even his own.

Bolan turned back to the defiant man. "Okay," he said. "We'll pay you to talk."

Ukewere smiled. "How much?"

"How much do you want?"

Ukewere looked at the ceiling, then back down. "That depends," he said finally. "What do you want to know?"

"I'm here to find the members of the Belgian theatrical troupe who were playing in Rwanda."

Ukewere's smile widened as he began to smell big money. "That will cost."

"Do you know where they are?"

The con man shook his head. "But I will find out if that's what you want." He paused. "For a mere one thousand American dollars."

The Executioner quickly thought about it. A thousand dollars wasn't particularly high for what he was asking, but a fortune in an impoverished nation like Rwanda.

Bolan shook his head. "No."

The hate returned to Ukewere's eyes. "Then I will not—"

"I'll give you *two* thousand dollars," the Executioner broke in. "But you stick with me until I find them, Ukewere."

The man's lips curled up at the corners, then his hand reached into his shirt pocket and grabbed two of the big cigars.

Still beaming, Ukewere handed one of the cigars to Walters and the other to Bolan, then jumped down off the chair to stand before the two men with his hands on his hips.

"Call me Sal, boys."

3

Cheap cigar smoke blew from the backseat of the rented Yugo, engulfing Bolan and Walters like giant blue-gray storm clouds. In the passenger's seat, the white-haired mercenary coughed, glanced at Bolan behind the wheel and shook his head before opening his window.

Behind them, between puffs on his cigar, Sal Ukewere continued the virtual one-sided conversation he'd begun since getting into the car. "And I can't say for sure that he knows Big Billy Rukanwe personally, but he'll know somebody who does and he's got a used-book store over on Travail—Librairie Travail, it's called—mostly French books that are hard to get or out of print, and of course most people can't afford books because of the war and food is more important, but he'd be doing pretty good even if that was *all* he did—which it's not. He sells information just like me and Tater here." He paused and drew a deep breath. "Right, Tater?"

Walters closed his eyes. "Right, Sal."

"Of course he runs in different circles than Tater and me, so he'll have different information, which is why we're going to see him. His name is Jean-Marc Mwisale, but I already told you that, didn't I?''

"Once or twice, Sal," Walters said, his eyes still closed against the nonstop verbal barrage that had begun as soon as Ukewere decided to talk.

Behind the wheel, Bolan chuckled softly as he followed a curve on Commerce Avenue. He reached under his jacket to adjust the leather shoulder rig Walters had provided with the S&W Model 629 .44 Magnum. The revolver rode well under his left arm, and although he'd have preferred the Desert Eagle in the same caliber, with the exception of holding only six rounds, the Smith did the same job.

The Browning Hi-Power was strapped to his right hip in a thumb-break holster, and the lightweight FEG .380 pistol the Executioner had appropriated earlier had been tucked into the right back pocket of his slacks.

The warrior's chuckle died abruptly as they entered the market area. The city was still enjoying a lull in the rioting, and the merchants were returning to do business with their meager goods. The Yugo drove slowly past stands that should have been packed with vegetables, live chickens and hanging sides of beef. Instead, Bolan saw only a scattered assortment of near-rotted foodstuffs that hadn't been purchased before the most recent outbreak of war, or were stolen during the pandemonium that followed.

Mixed throughout the edibles were vendors trying to hawk pottery, wall hangings, baskets and leather goods to nonexistent tourists, and natives who had no money. The overall atmosphere was one of poverty, starvation and despair. The people of Rwanda were dying, and if the fighting itself didn't kill them, the famine brought on by the war would.

"Turn right here," Ukewere said, "then pull in."

Bolan parked along the broken concrete curb in front of a hand-painted sign that read Librairie Travail. A moment later Ukewere led him and Walters through a splintered wooden door into the bookstore.

The Executioner surveyed the store as they walked down an aisle between bookshelves overflowing with secondhand volumes. Green paint chips from the walls covered the floor, and dust coated everything. A dead rat, its ribs visible against its sides, lay in the center of the aisle.

Ukewere stepped deftly over the carcass without a moment's pause and led Bolan and Walters to a desk at the rear of the room. The African came to a halt in front of a clerk who sat behind a disintegrating wooden desk.

The clerk looked up from behind the papers on his desk, his expression blank. Behind the desk, a black curtain hung from the ceiling over what the Executioner suspected was a doorway to the back office.

Ukewere's chest puffed out. "We are here to see Mr. Mwisale," he said in French.

The clerk just shook his head.

Ukewere's chin shot out. "Perhaps you did not hear me?"

"I heard you," the clerk replied. "Mr. Mwisale is not here."

"Do you not know who I am?" Ukewere asked.

A smile played at the corners of the clerk's thin lips as he shook his head again.

"I am Salewe Ukewere," he said indignantly, and waited.

When he got no response, Ukewere's eyes filled with the same hatred Bolan had seen at the hotel. "You would do well to learn who I am! Get Mr. Mwisale immediately!"

The curtain behind the desk moved to one side, and the largest man Bolan had seen since arriving in Rwanda stepped through the doorway. The skin of his face glistened with sweat above the open collar of his white sport shirt. He wore chocolate brown slacks, stood a good six and a half feet tall and had to have tipped the scales at three hundred pounds. The curtain fell closed behind him as he moved around the side of the desk toward Walters.

A moment later the curtain was thrown back again, and an even bigger man stooped under the seven-foot doorway to enter the room. Outweighing the first giant by a solid fifty pounds, this behemoth wore freshly pressed blue jeans and sparkling white athletic shoes. His hard eyes fell on Bolan as he circled the desk and stopped directly in front of the Executioner.

The man facing Walters spoke angrily in Kinyarwanda. Then his arms flashed out with lightning speed to encircle the white-haired mercenary and lift him off his feet in a spine-mangling bear hug.

The air rushed out of Walters's lungs, and he grunted, but the pain didn't stop him. He brought both hands out to his sides, palms open, then smashed them against the giant's ears.

The huge man screamed as he dropped the white-haired mercenary. His hands shot to his ears, but by then Walters had stepped back and directed a snap kick into his opponent's crotch. When his foot touched the ground, Walters used the other leg to sweep the giant's feet out from under him and sent him crashing to the floor.

The man in front of Bolan watched in shock, then growled like an angry bear and turned to the Executioner, reaching for his throat.

Bolan ducked the enormous hands and shot a short right jab into his attacker's sternum. His fist met both muscle and fat, weakening the effect of the punch. Raising a foot, he stomped hard on the enormous foot he saw below him, and heard a crack as his heel broke the man's instep.

The giant roared in agony, hopping up and down on one foot as Bolan stepped back. Without waiting for him to recover, the Executioner's foot shot out again, this time striking the knee of the bouncing leg. Another crack echoed against the walls of the bookstore, and the jumping giant fell to the floor next to his partner.

The clerk behind the desk stared in disbelief at the two men on the floor, his jaw dropping.

Ukewere stared at the man behind the desk and said, "Perhaps you did not understand me. Mr. Ukewere is here to see Mr. Mwisale."

Before the man could respond, the curtain opened again and a frail figure in a light green business suit stuck his head into the opening. Jean-Marc Mwisale had the complexion of the half French, half African. His features appeared to be mixed, as well, with wide lips below a sharp, narrow nose. He looked over the top of his reading glasses and shook his head in disgust, then glanced to Ukewere and waved him forward before disappearing behind the curtain once more.

Ukewere beamed triumphantly at Bolan, then circled the desk, threw open the curtain and strutted through the opening. The Executioner and Walters followed.

Mwisale led them down a dimly lit hallway, past the open door to his office, then to the next room. They entered a lounge area, its centerpiece a kitchen table surrounded by four matching chairs and a pair of wooden stools.

The bookstore proprietor pointed to the table, then moved to a coffee machine next to the sink in the counter at the rear of the room. Bolan and Walters took chairs as Ukewere took a seat on one of the stools.

Mwisale poured coffee into a plain white mug, didn't bother to offer them any, then took the other stool. "You appear to be coming up in the world, Sal," he said in French. "What can I do for you?"

Ukewere hooked his thumbs under his armpits and raised his chin a notch. "We are looking for Big Billy Rukanwe."

Mwisale reached up to adjust the glasses on his nose, and Bolan saw the diamonds sparkling on his fingers. "Good luck," he said. "Big Billy goes into hiding whenever fighting starts. Or so I hear."

"Do you know him?" Ukewere asked.

Mwisale shook his head.

"Do you know someone who does?"

"Of course," Mwisale said. "Everyone knows someone who links to everyone in the world. The trick is to organize that information and put it into—" he let his voice trail off and looked at Bolan "—a *marketable* form." Glancing back to Ukewere, he added, "Some do it more successfully than others, and therefore they charge more."

The petition for payment was all too obvious. The Executioner stared Mwisale in the eye. The bookstore owner and his two henchmen looked like the only three men in Rwanda who weren't starving. And the reason for that was as obvious as the man's solicitation.

Mwisale grew fat at the expense of the less fortunate, and the Executioner resented contributing anything to someone like that. But he needed any information the bookstore owner might have that could lead him to Dusty Morrison and the rest of the performers.

"If it's good information," Bolan said, "I'll pay."

"It will cost you fifty thousand Rwandan francs."

"It will cost me ten thousand Rwandan francs," the Executioner stated.

"Forty thousand."

"Twenty thousand, and that's the last offer," Bolan said, his eyes still locked to Mwisale's. "Say no to that, and I'll leave you on the floor next to your goons in the front room."

Mwisale smiled again. "You drive a hard bargain."

The warrior nodded. "Start talking or you'll find out just how hard it can get."

The bookstore owner nodded back in understanding, pulled a spiral notepad and pen from the inside pocket of his sport coat and scribbled a name and address on the page before tearing it out and pushing it across the table to the Executioner.

Bolan glanced at the paper, then stuck it in his pocket and stood.

Mwisale continued to grin. "Aren't you forgetting something?" he said.

"No," Bolan said. "I haven't forgotten." Reaching into his pocket, he pulled out a roll of Rwandan francs and slowly counted off the payment before returning the rest to his pocket.

The warrior's hand shot out suddenly, grabbing Mwisale's necktie. He twisted it around his hand, tightening the knot at the bookseller's throat until the man's eyes threatened to pop from the sockets. Mwisale's mouth gaped open, struggling for air.

The Executioner used the tie to drag the man across the room to the door. Walters and Ukewere followed him down the dark hallway, back into the bookstore and over the still-moaning men on the floor. Bolan used his free hand to open the door to the street and pulled Mwisale out to the sidewalk.

A light breeze ruffled the Executioner's hair as he looked up and down the street. To his right he saw a man and woman, arm in arm, helping each other limp down the sidewalk.

The Executioner turned to the frightened man whose tie he still gripped. "You're about to do the first good deed you've ever done, Mwisale," he said. Then, dropping the man, he stepped into the path of the two Rwandans.

The couple looked up, their eyes glazed with hunger.

Bolan pulled a thousand francs off the top of the bills in his hand and pressed them into the palm of the emaciated man, who looked up at him in awe.

Then the Executioner turned back to Mwisale, and as the book dealer watched in horror, he lifted his hand over his head and released the rest of the money into the wind.

DENISE LEFEVRE DRIED herself with a towel, wrapped it around her head and took a seat on the vanity bench in front of the mirror. Staring at her nude reflection, she fought the melancholy that always threatened to overtake her whenever she applied her makeup. Her eyes made their way from the crow's-feet at the corner of the sockets to the ever-deepening creases around her mouth, and finally to the loose skin beneath her chin.

Throwing back her shoulders, the actress thrust out her breasts. At least they didn't sag yet. Her hand traveled to her stomach and over her abdomen. The muscles were still firm, but more difficult to see these days no matter how many sit-ups she did or how strictly she kept to her diet.

LeFevre sighed. She exercised harder than ever, spending hours on the machines and more at the ballet bar. She stretched, she ran, she ate less than her pet parakeet. Yet she couldn't stop the aging process.

A knock on the other side of the bathroom door shook her from her misery. "Denise? Are you all right in there?" Hubert Spaak's voice asked with forced theatrical concern.

LeFevre composed herself quickly. "I'm fine, Hubert," she lied. "Leave me alone."

"I was just concerned." Spaak's footfalls moved off down the hall.

LeFevre turned to the door, picturing the young man who had just stood on the other side. Hubert Spaak was concerned, all right, but not for her welfare. He was concerned with getting her into bed. The egotistical little brat was reputed to have slept with every leading lady he'd ever made a movie with, and he was afraid that if he didn't bed Denise LeFevre during this African tour, word might leak out that his string of conquests had been broken.

The actress turned back to the mirror. She couldn't deny that Hubert was handsome. The fact that he found her attractive, and still in the same league as the young starlets in his movies, was flattering. It did a little, at least, to offset the depression that flooded her each time she put on her makeup.

Which was what she was there to do, she reminded herself. Put on her makeup and try to cover up the fact that she was forty-three years old and not ageless like Sophia Loren.

Opening her makeup case, the middle-aged actress congratulated herself for having it nearby when the fighting had broken out. But then, it was never far from hand these days. She applied a coat of base, some blush and powder, then lifted the mascara wand and began to brush her eyelashes, her thoughts returning to Hubert Spaak.

She had considered sleeping with him at first to relieve the boredom of the tour. Then she had considered it to remind herself that despite a few wrinkles she was still appealing to younger men. But then the fighting had broken out, and the next thing she knew they were all living like sardines in this underground hiding place.

LeFevre put down the mascara and lifted her lipstick, applying a coat to her lips, then blotting them together. She supposed she should be thankful for the fighting, in a perverse way. It had kept her from becoming another notch on Spaak's zipper. Kept him from bedding her, then moving on to greener—read that younger—pastures.

Twisting the lid of her eye shadow, the woman suddenly stopped. There were no greener pastures here, she suddenly realized. She was the only woman, young or old, beautiful or homely. She looked back to the mirror. The sudden knowledge, combined with the fresh makeup, made her feel a little better. She didn't know how long they'd have to hide down here before the fighting let up and they could get out of the country, but until then she was the queen.

Another knock on the bathroom door interrupted her thoughts.

"Denise!" Streak shouted. "If you don't come out this instant, I'll have an accident!"

"Put a rubber band around it," LeFevre suggested, and went back to her makeup. She caught herself smiling into the mirror. Finishing with her mascara, she brushed her hair, then stood and turned around. Her mood elevated now, she looked into the mirror, and even the sight of the little dimples forming in her buttocks didn't bring her mood down. She turned sideways, staring critically at the glass.

Okay, her body wasn't what it had once been. But she still had a damn fine ass. At least directors still wanted to expose it on screen every time they could talk her into it. It would do for another few years, at least.

LeFevre was slipping into a clean pair of panties when a third knock came to the door.

"Yes?" she said, exasperated.

"Oh . . . sorry."

For a second she didn't recognize the voice. Then it dawned on her. Dusty Morrison.

"I'll just be a second," she said, changing her tone to a friendlier note, but the lack of reply told her Morrison had already left.

The actress shrugged into a clean bra and reached behind her back to fasten it. She frowned, caught the expression in the mirror, reminded herself that frowning was like fertilizer to wrinkles and let her face fall deadpan. Dusty Morrison. Tall and strong, he nevertheless had to be close to sixty years old. He still looked sexy in his cowboy clothes, though, and she found herself strangely attracted to him.

Pulling a T-shirt over her head, LeFevre reached for the jeans she'd laid out on the counter next to the sink. In her late teens and early twenties she'd been attracted to older men—father figures, she supposed. Then, as she got older herself, she'd found herself attracted to younger men like Spaak.

LeFevre stuck her feet into the pant legs of her jeans. It didn't take a Ph.D. in psychology to figure out why. Seducing men twenty years younger than she was kept her feeling young herself.

So what was it she liked about Morrison?

She wiggled the tight denim jeans up her hips, picturing Dusty Morrison onstage, drawing his—what did he call them—six-shooters, and blasting away. He was more than just show, too. He'd proved that by shooting for real when they were making their escape.

Taking a final look in the mirror, the actress concluded that what she saw wasn't as good as it had been when she'd been twenty. But for forty-three it wasn't bad at all. She turned to the door, reached out for the knob, then stopped.

Was she going to let Hubert Spaak have his way to relieve the stress and boredom of their predicament, or would it be more fun to continue to lead him around by a leash? She didn't know yet. Maybe that was what made it fun.

She opened the door and stepped out into the hall.

All three men were waiting in line, with Dusty Morrison at the end. Ignoring Streak and Spaak, Denise LeFevre gave the gray-haired cowboy her best smile as she passed on her way back to the living room.

If only Dusty weren't so old.

And if only she weren't, either.

THE EXECUTIONER HEARD the match strike behind him and then smoke began to fill the vehicle once more.

Tater Walters turned toward him, sighed and rolled down the window again.

"Hamissi Karuzi, yeah, I know him, not real well, but I know who he is," Ukewere said around the cigar in his mouth. "Muslim. Works over at the Snack Tam-Tam." He stopped suddenly. "Hey, where are my manners, right? Anybody else want a cigar?"

Bolan shook his head.

Walters rolled the window down farther and said, "I don't need my own, Sal. I'll just breathe in what you exhale."

The man ignored the remark. "Take a right and park in here, Collier," he said, jabbing at the window with his cigar.

Bolan twisted the steering wheel, guiding the vehicle off Revolution and onto a lot scattered with the remains of a building. Brick and concrete rubble littered the area, and two corners of the structure were the only parts still intact. Weeds and grass grew through the cracks in the foundation.

The Executioner cut the engine and got out, following Ukewere, who led him and Walters back to the sidewalk, then two storefronts down to a sign that read Snack Tam-Tam. A half dozen iron tables, their white paint chipped and cracked, stood outside the door on the pavement. A middle-aged couple wearing cameras around their neck were the café's only patrons. Both sat with their backs to the building and nervously tried to eat.

Watching them as he pulled a chair away from the table Ukewere had chosen, Bolan realized that like Dusty Morrison and the Belgians, these people had to have entered the country before the war broke out again. They had probably been holed up in a nearby hotel for the past couple of days before hunger finally forced them out.

Bolan took a seat as the door to the building opened and a man wearing white slacks, a white T-shirt and a white waiter's jacket came out carrying a pitcher of ice tea. The man's features were distinctly Arabic, and his tight curly hair was close-cropped to his skull. He walked briskly to the couple at the other table, then glanced toward the three newcomers as he refilled their glasses.

The Arab did a double take when he saw Ukewere.

The little man leaned across the table. "That's him," he whispered. "That is Karuzi."

Hurrying back inside the restaurant, Karuzi returned a moment later with a pen and order pad. He glanced nervously up and down the street before moving in between Walters and Ukewere. "What will you have?" he asked in French.

"Information," Ukewere answered in the same language.

Karuzi leaned in closer. "Not here," he said. "These are dangerous times. Order something and I will meet you later."

"Pizza," Ukewere said. "Extra large. Double ham and sausage."

Karuzi grimaced, but wrote it down.

Ukewere turned to face Bolan and Walters, waiting for them to order, letting them know the pizza was for him alone.

The two men both ordered sandwiches. Karuzi added them to his list, then disappeared back into the building.

Ukewere laughed. "The ham," he said. "He is Muslim and does not approve of eating pork."

Karuzi reappeared ten minutes later carrying a large round pizza pan. Steam rose from the sizzling cheese, ham and sausage, and Bolan noted that Karuzi had put on padded gloves.

Ukewere licked his lips as he stared at the platter in front of him. Karuzi set small baskets in front of Bolan and Walters and started to turn.

The little man tore his attention away from the pizza long enough to grab the Arab's arm. "You said you would meet us," he said. "Where? And when?"

"I finish work in thirty minutes," he said.

By now Ukewere had lifted a piece of the pizza to his mouth with his free hand and torn a huge bite off with his teeth. The heat didn't seem to bother him as he spoke and chewed at the same time. "Then we will meet you at the bar in the Sierra," he said, pointing over his shoulder.

Bolan glanced down the street and saw the sign.

Karuzi shook his head. "That is too close and I am known there. Make it the Good Times on Travail."

Ukewere took another bite. "Too far," he said.

"It is there or nowhere." Karuzi jerked his arm away and hurried back into the building.

As soon as they'd finished their meal, the Executioner pulled several Rwandan bills from his pocket, weighted them down with the basket his sandwich had come in and stood. He led the way back to the car, slid behind the wheel and retraced the route they had taken from Travail. He parked along the curb, then Ukewere led him and Walters down a small lane off the main street.

The African opened the door, stepped back graciously and ushered the other men inside. "The prices here are good," he said. "Much better than the Snack Tam-Tam."

A waiter led them to a window table in the main bar, and the Executioner took a seat where he could see both the door and the sidewalk outside.

"I am still hungry," Ukewere said, then turned to the waiter. He ordered another pizza and a pitcher of beer.

Bolan and Walters settled for beer.

Ukewere had finished the second pizza by the time Karuzi appeared on the sidewalk outside the window. The Arab had discarded his jacket but still wore the white slacks and T-shirt. He had added a black-and-white-striped *keffiyeh*. Not changing habits, he looked up and down the street before ducking into the restaurant.

Bolan pulled out the chair next to him. Karuzi approached cautiously, his eyes searching the room as he walked. He took the seat as their waiter approached the table again, and ordered coffee.

"We are trying to locate Big Billy Rukanwe," Ukewere said without preamble. "We will pay."

Karuzi shook his head. "I do not know the man."

Bolan leaned in, crossing his arms on the table in front of him. "But you know who he is," he said matter-of-factly.

"Of course. He is an entertainment promoter. His most recent venture was the booking of the Belgian show traveling across Africa." He paused, turned to look behind him, then faced the others again. "It is rumored that they are still in the country. When they are found—either by Hutu *or* Tutsi—they will be killed."

Bolan nodded. "There's an American with them."

Karuzi looked him in the eye. "The cowboy. I saw the show. That is why you have come? To rescue him?"

"And the others." Bolan reached into his pocket and pulled out the roll of Rwandan bills. Peeling off the top three, he dropped them on the table and said, "Tell me how to find Rukanwe."

The Arab snatched the money off the table and jammed it into his pants pocket. "I know a man who is a friend of Big Billy's."

Bolan waited.

Karuzi looked down at the money in the Executioner's hand. The warrior counted off five more bills.

"I used to work for this man, this friend of Rukanwe's," the Arab said. "He is half-Hutu. His father was Jordanian." He looked back down at the money.

The Executioner gave him five additional notes.

"He is an exporter of coffee and tea."

"Where? Here in Kigali?"

The Arab shook his head. "His business is near Cyangugu."

This time when Karuzi looked at the money, Bolan counted out ten bills, dropped them on the table and said, "I'm tired of playing this game. Take this. It's all you get. So start talking." He let the tone of his voice imply what would happen if the Arab continued to be difficult.

Karuzi took the hint. "Zaid Karsimbi is his name. Ukewere will have heard of him."

The little man nodded. "Tea and coffee," he agreed. "Among other things."

Karuzi turned his eyes toward Bolan. "Yes. Karsimbi is involved in many investments. Some legal, some not so. He exports coffee and tea. His imports include drugs, such as *khat*."

Bolan listened. *Khat,* grown primarily in Kenya, was a mild drug that produced amphetaminelike reactions. While it was more prevalent in African countries with better economies, the people of Rwanda needed an "escape" as much as anyone, maybe more.

Regardless of how impoverished a nation might be, some people always found money for drugs.

"Be careful if you go to see him," Karuzi said. "He will be nervous during these times. His bodyguards will shoot first and ask questions later, as you Americans like to say." He tried looking down at the money again but Bolan ignored him, shoving the bills back into his pocket. Producing a pen from a jacket pocket, he grabbed a cocktail napkin and pushed them both toward Karuzi. "Write down the directions," he ordered.

Karuzi complied, then all four men stood.

Karuzi cleared his throat. "I have given you good information?" he asked.

Bolan nodded.

"I . . . could use more money," he said shyly.

The Executioner fished into his pocket, pulled out another bill and dropped it on the table. He thought briefly of Mwisale. "If you want more," he said, "try looking up and down the street. Who knows? There might still be a few francs blowing in the wind."

As he turned to leave he saw a look of bewilderment come over the Arab's face.

4

Dusty Morrison watched Denise LeFevre walk into the living room, thought of Lois and frowned.

What was it about Denise that always made him think of his wife? She didn't look like Lois. She didn't walk or talk like Lois, and she certainly didn't act like Lois. Denise was a little on the affected side. Each word, each movement, was carefully played out as if it came from a well-rehearsed script. Lois, on the other hand, had been the most genuine human being he'd ever known. What you saw was what you got.

Morrison watched Streak hurry into the bathroom holding his groin like a little kid. A moment later the sound of urine splashing against the side of the toilet bowl drifted through the door. His mind still on Lois, Morrison leaned back against the wall, turned toward the living room and looked past LeFevre, who had taken a seat on one of the couches.

The living room made the actor think of a place he and Lois had rented one winter in the Bahamas. But in the same sense that he couldn't figure out why Denise LeFevre always made him think of his wife, he couldn't understand why this underground dwelling brought that Caribbean beach house to mind. The floor plan was completely different, and the furniture in the Bahamas had been those big basket-looking tables and chair. There was a name for them and Lois could always remember it when he couldn't.

Morrison felt himself frowning again as he continued to stare into the living room. Distantly he heard the toilet flush, then the water in the sink began to run. A voice to his side said, "Don't waste your time even thinking about it, pops."

The voice jolted the cowboy actor from his reverie. He turned to see Hubert Spaak grinning at him, and suddenly realized, with considerable embarrassment, that Spaak thought his gaze had been directed at Denise.

Morrison started to speak, but Spaak gave him an all-knowing we're-both-men-of-the-world look and nodded toward the living room. "I've got that one all sewed up," Spaak said. "Just a matter of time before I've got her spread across the bed in there." He glanced toward the larger of the two bedrooms, then looked back and showed Morrison all of his perfectly capped teeth. "Want to lay a little money down on how long it takes me?" He chuckled vulgarly.

Morrison's eyes narrowed as he looked at the pathetically shallow young movie star. "You've got a lot to learn, kid," he said softly.

Spaak threw back his head and the chuckle turned to a cackle. "Maybe," he said. "But not from a second-rate B-movie has-been."

The door opened and Streak walked into the hall. Spaak turned and disappeared into the bathroom. A few minutes later the toilet flushed, then the door opened and Spaak strutted out.

"I can think of at least one thing you could learn from a has-been like me," Morrison said as he pushed past the man.

"Yeah, pops? What's that?" Spaak asked, laughing.

"To wash your hands after you use the bathroom." Morrison closed the door as the smirk fell from Spaak's face.

Finishing his business, Morrison washed his hands, dried them on the towel hanging next to the sink and opened the door.

A deathlike quiet had crept over the house. Morrison noticed it as soon as he stepped out into the hall. Moving silently along the carpet, he turned the corner into the living room and saw the others frozen to their seats. Their gazes were locked on to the ceiling of the underground living room.

From overhead came footsteps and muffled voices.

The aging cowboy kicked himself mentally. Earlier in the day he'd been reading a poorly written Western novel and suddenly wondered if someone on top would be able to hear the toilet flush. He'd made a mental note to tell the others that a quick check through the periscope should precede all bathroom visits.

Then the novel had put him to sleep in his chair, and he'd forgotten all about it. Until now.

Holding his index finger to his lips, Morrison moved back into the hallway and slowly opened the door to the utility closet. He leaned into the periscope, closing one eye.

In the tiny mirror, he saw two men. Both were black, and both wore the worn and faded green BDUs of the Tutsi-controlled army. Assault rifles were slung over their shoulders.

He started to turn the periscope, then decided against it. He didn't know exactly where the periscope came out of the ground, and even that slight movement might be seen. Besides, he knew all he needed to know.

Armed men were directly above them, and it didn't matter how many. Even two were too many for the fourteen rounds of weak bird shot that still remained in his single-action Peacemakers and the loops on his Buscadero rig.

By the time Morrison got back to the living room, Denise LeFevre was standing in front of Streak. "You must go to the door and try to hear!" she whispered, grasping both his shoulders. "You're the only one who understands the language. You must see if you can understand what they are saying!"

Streak sat frozen in an overstuffed easy chair, his hands like frozen claws on the arms. He didn't move.

Spaak rose suddenly and stepped between Streak and LeFevre. "Get up! Get your ass up to that door and find out what they know!"

When Streak didn't move, Spaak glanced at LeFevre, then slapped the makeup artist across the face.

Tears began to flow down Streak's cheeks. His chest heaved from both fear and humiliation, but his fingers still gripped the chair.

Spaak's open hand moved back again.

Morrison stepped in behind Spaak and caught the arm before it could strike again. Spaak spun toward him, his other hand balling into a fist.

Morrison shook his head. "That's enough."

Spaak stared at him, his eyes fiery with rage. Then his fist relaxed and he turned to spit on the floor.

The cowboy actor moved in and leaned over the man in the chair. "Streak," he whispered. "Streak!"

The terrified man looked up.

"We need your help, pard. Denise is right. You're the only one who knows the lingo." He paused, took the man's frail arm and pulled him gently to his feet. Still holding the arm, Morrison guided Streak across the living room and up the steps to the door. "It'll be all right if we're quiet," he whispered. "It'll be all right, Streak."

The two men stopped just below the door. The makeup artist stretched upward, twisting his neck and pressing his ear against the door. For several minutes Morrison waited, then he heard the sound of footsteps fade away.

Streak was still shaking when he turned to the aging cowboy. The older man shook his head, held his finger to his lips again, then guided the makeup man back down the stairs.

By the time they returned to the living room, Streak could speak again. He dropped into the same chair he'd been in before, looked at the floor, then up again. "I've got some good news and some bad news," he whispered as if the men were still directly above them. "The good news is, they've left."

Morrison, LeFevre and Spaak waited in silence.

"The bad news," Streak finally said, "is that they heard the toilet. They're coming back with more men . . . and a metal detector."

SCATTERED GUNSHOTS exploded in the distance as Bolan, Walters and Ukewere left the bar. Two blocks down from where the Yugo was parked, the Executioner saw a young man slam a brick through a window.

A moment later he and a dozen other young men began carrying boxes out of the store like a well-organized army of ants.

Bolan slid behind the wheel again and pulled the vehicle out onto Travail. "You don't happen to have a plane handy?" he asked Walters, knowing the answer before he asked.

The mercenary shook his head. "I can get one, though," he said. "Give me a day, two, tops—"

"I can have one this afternoon," Ukewere said from the backseat as he lit another cigar. "But it will be very expensive."

"We don't have time for either," Bolan said as he angled around the corner toward Commerce. "Is there a shuttle from Kigali to Cyangugu?"

Walters nodded. "Air Rwanda goes to Kamembe, which is close by. But there's no guarantee they'll be operating." As if to prove his point, another shot rang out in the distance. The merc patted his .45s. "And there'll be metal detectors."

Bolan nodded, silently wishing that he'd brought along Jack Grimaldi, the ace pilot from Stony Man Farm. But Grimaldi was currently tied up with Phoenix Force, and even if he hadn't been, the mission the Executioner had undertaken was in direct violation of a presidential order. The fewer people he pulled out on the limb with him, the better.

The warrior followed a curve in the road past Place de l'Unité Nationale and onto Boulevard de Ioa, starting toward the airport.

Behind the Executioner, Ukewere cleared his throat. "We'll be going past the Umagnanura restaurant," he said. "You can just pay me and let me out there."

Bolan shook his head. "Not on a bet."

"What do you mean?" Ukewere said. "I've done my part. Karsimbi will tell you where Rukanwe is."

"Maybe," the warrior said, speeding up to pass a slow-moving panel van. To the side of the road, he saw a band of roving youths carrying captured submachine guns. "But the deal was, you stick with us until we've found Rukanwe."

The little man shot forward, sticking his head over the seat. "Bullshit!" he cried. "The deal didn't include chasing down somebody like Zaid Karsimbi. You know who he is?"

Bolan shrugged. "I take it he's a coffee and tea exporter and runs some drugs as a sideline."

"Yeah, but it's one hell of a sideline. *Khat* isn't all he's involved in. Believe it or not, there are a few people in this country who can afford heroin and cocaine—at least crack. Karsimbi's behind it all."

When the Executioner didn't answer, Ukewere turned to Walters. "Tell him, Tater," he demanded.

Walters looked at Bolan and shrugged. "He's right. Karsimbi looks respectable enough on the surface, but to those in the know, he's the local Mafia. The little bastard's a candy-ass himself, but he's got some mean mothers working for him. Anything else you want me to tell him, Sal?" he asked with only a trace of sarcasm.

"Yeah, you can tell him that if we go see Karsimbi he'll have us all killed."

Walters chuckled. "I can do that, Sal, but I don't get the feeling it'll change his mind." He turned back to Bolan and said, "He wants me to tell you that if we go see—"

"I heard him," the Executioner said. He turned onto the road leading to the airport. "We're going to see him, anyway."

Walters looked back at Ukewere and shrugged again, then faced the front as they neared the remains of a burned-out motel.

"Wrong," Ukewere said. "You're crazy and I'm not going." He paused, then said, "Let me out here."

Bolan pulled into the motel parking lot and stopped.

Ukewere waited a good thirty seconds, then said, "Well?"

"Well what?" Bolan asked.

"I want my money."

"Then you'll have to earn it," the Executioner replied.

"Dammit, Collier!" Ukewere said. "I'm not going!"

"Then you aren't getting paid."

Ukewere looked around exasperated, then pounded his fists on the top of the seat. "Okay," he said in frustration. "I offered to give you information to get you started for a thousand dollars. You said two thousand if I stayed with you."

"That's right," Bolan agreed.

"I've got you started. Just give me the thousand and I'll be on my way."

"That wasn't the deal."

Ukewere threw himself backward against the seat and cut loose with another string of Kinyarwanda curses that Bolan didn't have to understand to grasp the intent.

Walters looked at the Executioner. "I won't translate directly, but he's being extremely creative in what he'd like to see happen between you and several large jungle animals."

Bolan laughed and turned to drape his arm over the seat. By now Ukewere had quieted and sat pouting. "You getting out or staying?" the Executioner asked.

The African took a deep breath. "Let's go."

The warrior threw the Yugo back in gear and pulled out of the parking lot. A few minutes later he turned into the lot next to the terminal. One look at the front door told him that Air Rwanda wouldn't be keeping to its schedule this day. A riot had broken out, with some men and women scurrying out of the terminal while others traded punches along the sidewalk.

Cutting the wheel toward the landing strips, Bolan cruised along the runway until he saw an open hangar in the distance. A white man in a bright yellow shirt and white slacks was pulling what looked like a Beechcraft Baron out the front door.

Hitting the accelerator, the Executioner sped toward the hangar.

"We doing what I think we're doing?" Walters asked.

Bolan nodded. "Don't kill him."

The Executioner screeched the Yugo to a halt next to the Beechcraft and leaped out, the Smith & Wesson 629 extended in his hand.

The man in the yellow shirt froze. His hands rose into the air without his being told. "Don't shoot!" he said in a clipped British accent. "I've got room for you all."

Bolan realized that like so many others in Rwanda, visitor and native alike, this man just wanted out of the country. And he assumed that was what the three men in the Yugo wanted, too.

Dropping the .44 Magnum gun to arm's length, he smiled. "Then get her warmed up."

As the riot in front of the terminal grew and the Beechcraft's engines purred, the Executioner learned that the pilot was originally from Southampton, England, but had been living in South Africa for the past several years. His name was Bradfordson.

"Call me Art," Bradfordson said.

Ten minutes later Bolan, Walters and Ukewere climbed aboard the Beechcraft Baron and strapped themselves into their seats.

Bradfordson pulled a brown leather bomber hat over his head and buckled the chin strap. "Off we go, chappies," he said as the Beechcraft taxied forward. "We'll be away from this nonsense and tucked in bed in Johannesburg by nightfall." He turned to Bolan next to him and exhibited a toothy grin. "Yanks, I assume?" he said. "Except for the Twa, of course."

The Executioner nodded.

Bradfordson guided the plane into the air, leveled it off a few hundred feet above the ground, then extended his hand across the seat. "Always happy to help out fellow travelers."

Bolan shook his hand.

"You blokes ever been to South Africa?" Bradford asked over the roar of the engines.

The Executioner nodded. "Once or twice."

Bradfordson pulled a scratched brier pipe and a leather pouch from the pocket of his white slacks, stuck the pipe in his mouth and began to fill it with tobacco. "Well, a hundred quid say I'll be taking you to some spots tonight you've never found in your tourist brochures."

The Executioner smiled. He liked Bradfordson. "I'd take that bet," he said, "but it wouldn't be fair. We aren't going to Johannesburg. At least not tonight. Tonight we'll be in Cyangugu."

Bradfordson dipped a wing, turning the Beechcraft due south. He turned to Bolan as the Executioner opened his jacket to expose the big stainless-steel revolver in the shoulder holster.

The Briton frowned as he turned in his seat, looked down at the .44 Magnum weapon, then up at the Executioner. Then the frown disappeared, he shrugged and said, "Cyangugu it is, then, mates!"

A moment later the Beechcraft Baron had angled to the southwest.

SAL UKEWERE REVIVED his campaign to get out of going to see Karsimbi, switching tactics as the plane began to descend over Cyangugu. "You don't need me," he said. "I'll just be in the way. If you don't want to pay me now, I'll wait here with the plane."

Bolan turned in his seat and shook his head. "No, Sal. I think you'd better come with us."

"Why? I can't help you."

"Maybe I just like your company," the Executioner said. "But on the other hand, I suspect that if I let you out of my sight I won't see you again."

Turning to Bradfordson, the Executioner asked, "You know this area very well?"

The pilot shrugged. "Fairly."

"I don't want to land at the airport," the Executioner said. "Is there a strip of flat land anywhere close to town where we could set her down?"

Bradfordson frowned. "I've never tried it before, but there *is* a band of land just to the south that I suspect will serve our purposes.'' He turned to the Executioner and smiled.

Bolan suppressed his own grin. It had become apparent that while the man was still a little frightened of what was happening to him, he was getting off on the adventure of it all, as well. The warrior had learned more about the Briton during the flight from Kigali.

Bradfordson came from old London money, and although he spoke of businesses in Pretoria, Cape Town and Johannesburg, Bolan had read between the lines. Bradfordson was pretty much an international playboy whose main occupation was safari hunting and hanging out in the more colorful bars up and down the continent. His business ventures seemed simply to justify a certain guilt complex for being born with no actual need to work.

''You don't understand what it's like,'' Ukewere whispered.

The Executioner turned back to the African. The little man was staring at his feet, his face looking crestfallen. ''Okay, Sal,'' Bolan said, sighing. ''What is it I don't understand?''

Ukewere looked up. ''You don't understand what it's like to be little.''

''No,'' Bolan said. ''I guess I don't. I can't imagine what it's like to be little—either physically or emotionally. But there's one thing I do understand that I don't think you know I do, Sal.''

Ukewere's eyes widened slightly. ''What?''

"That the Belgian theater troupe we're looking for aren't the only professional actors in Rwanda." Pausing to let it sink in, the Executioner went on. "Sal, cut the crap with me. I don't buy it." He looked out the window again and saw a flat stretch of grassland a hundred feet below the descending Beechcraft. "And like I said, being small in stature doesn't give you the right to be a small person, if you get my drift."

Ukewere exploded as the wheels hit the grass. "You son of a bitch!" he shouted. "You think you're so damn smart! You think you can see through anything, don't you?"

Bolan shrugged. "Weak and transparent con jobs have never been a problem." He turned back to the front, watching the African in the mirror attached to the visor.

Fiery daggers shot from Ukewere's eyes into the back of Bolan's skull. "Fuck you!" he cried. "Just fuck you!" He drew a deep breath that threatened to pop the buttons off his shirt. "Let me tell you something, Mr. Six-foot-whatever and Two-hundred Pounds. You *don't* know what it's like to be a Twa in Rwanda. You *don't* know what it's like to come home one day and find that soldiers have cut your whole family to pieces with machetes, either!" His mouth clamped shut suddenly as if he'd revealed something he hadn't meant to.

The words hit the Executioner hard. His mind shot back over the years, to the home in which he'd grown up. Suddenly he was standing in the living room again, in the uniform of a U.S. Army Special Forces sergeant.

And the bloodstains were still on the carpet.

Turning to face Sal Ukewere, Bolan looked into the man's hate-filled eyes. "You're right," he said. "*My* father, mother and little sister had been dead two days by the time I got there. Their bodies had already been removed."

Ukewere's lower lip dropped open. "Murdered? Your family, too?"

Bolan nodded.

Distrust entered the man's eyes. "You're just saying that."

Bolan continued to stare at Ukewere. "I wish I were," he said.

By now the Beechcraft had taxied to a halt. The Executioner felt Walters's and Bradfordson's eyes on him as an uneasy silence fell over the cabin of the aircraft.

The Executioner turned back to the front of the plane, took a deep breath, then opened the door. "Let's go," he said. "We've got work to do."

TATER WALTERS ADJUSTED the twin .45 Government Model pistols against his kidneys as he stepped down from the Beechcraft. The white-haired mercenary fell in behind Ukewere and Bradfordson. The man who called himself Collier led them across the grass toward the cracked asphalt they'd seen from the air. The road was thick with slow-walking pedestrians on their way to the refugee camp in Bukavu. They were Hutus mainly, since at least for the moment the Tutsis were taking their turn in Rwanda's driver's seat. He hadn't seen any cars or trucks on the road, and if there were any, they'd be heading in the wrong direction.

The aging mercenary grinned. That meant either a march or double time over the two miles between them and the city. Which was fine with him. He'd kept in good shape over the years and could still outrun most men half his age.

Bolan stopped at the edge of the asphalt and looked both ways. Walters followed his gaze. Scattered along both sides of the road were groups of emaciated Hutus trudging away from the city in the hope of reaching the border before starvation, dehydration or Tutsi troops cut them down.

The big man turned to face Walters. "Any chance of a car coming by on its way in?" he asked, nodding toward Cyangugu.

Walters shrugged. "It's unlikely. Everybody who's out wants to go the other way. And even if something comes by, they aren't going to stop for guys who look like us."

Bolan's jaw set tight as he nodded his understanding.

A man, woman and three children limped up to them, and the four men stepped out of their way to let them pass. The family didn't seem to notice as they plodded on with transfixed eyes.

The Executioner glanced from Bradfordson to Ukewere, then back to Walters. "Then we'll have to hoof it," he said. "Bring up the rear, Tater. Make sure these two keep up."

Walters nodded and fell back behind Bradfordson and Ukewere.

Bolan turned his back and broke into a jog.

Walters followed Bradfordson and Ukewere as they began trotting along the grassy shoulder of the road. They zigzagged around more groups of fleeing refugees as they ran, the hot sun beating down unmercifully. They hadn't gone a hundred yards before sweat broke out on the white-haired merc's forehead. He watched Ukewere's short legs driving forward like pistons, and the sight brought another grin across his wrinkled features. The Twa could run better than he'd have guessed, even if his small legs had to take two steps for every one Bradfordson took beside him.

A few drops of sweat rolled through Walters's eyebrows and fell down his face. He wiped the back of his arm across his forehead as he ran, feeling himself fall into the steady, easy lope that meant his aging muscles were starting to warm up. He'd known Collier only a few short hours now, but he knew him well. He'd known many like him over the years.

No, he didn't know the details of John Collier's life, but he could guess. Military experience, definitely. It was hard to tell exactly how old he was, because like Walters himself, he kept fit. But he suspected Collier had done a tour or two in the Nam, and from the confidence the big man exuded, Special Forces was a likely possibility. Collier was a loner by nature—independent as hell—that was obvious. Which meant he'd more than likely specialized in demo work or been a sniper. Yeah, he could picture that. Imagining Collier moving silently through the bush with a scoped M-14, his face streaked with combat cosmestics, wasn't hard. It fit.

Ahead, Walters could hear Bradfordson breathing harder. They'd covered about a half mile so far, and it was obvious the playboy Briton spent more time in bars than he did at the gym. But Collier had increased the pace considerably after the first quarter mile, and Bradfordson wasn't really doing all that bad.

It was Ukewere who surprised him. The little man's legs were still flashing steadily along, his short arms moving back and forth. He was breathing easily around the unlit cigar in his teeth, while Walters would have guessed he'd have passed out alongside the road by now.

The white-haired merc looked up again as Collier cut around a half dozen ragtag Hutus hobbling along the roadway. The big man didn't even break stride, and Ukewere and Bradfordson followed his lead. Walters cut over behind them.

What would a man like Collier have done after Vietnam? Walters wondered. Maybe like Walters himself, he'd been recruited by the CIA. Hell, he might still be with them. Maybe this rescue was a Company deal.

More sweat dripped from his brows into his eyes, and Walters ran his arm across his face, blinking. No, Brognola was his contact, and Brognola was with the Justice Department. And somehow he couldn't see

Collier as a trench-coat spook. The tight-assed politi-
cian supervisors in their ties and suits would have had
even more trouble controlling the big man than they'd
had keeping tabs on Walters.

Was Collier an independent merc? Maybe. A distinct possibility. He still had the bearing of a soldier.
But if he'd hit the mercenary trail, Walters suspected
that John Collier would have been one of the "picky"
ones, accepting assignments only from benefactors
whom he agreed with politically.

Walters ran on. And what was that about the big
man's family? They'd been murdered? Knowing the
kind of man Collier was, he suspected those murders
hadn't gone unavenged. That whole deal had him curious as hell, but he had no intention of asking about
it. It was the kind of thing a man talked about if, and
when, he wanted to, and Collier wasn't the type who'd
need any half-assed, politically correct touchy-feely
"support group."

The runners started up a long rolling hill, and
Bradfordson began to fall back. Walters slowed as
Ukewere moved on. Fifty yards ahead, near the top of
the rise now, the white-haired merc could see Collier
still running at what looked like a leisurely pace.

Bradfordson dropped back next to him, his chest
heaving for air. Walters grinned again. "Getting tired,
Art?" he asked.

The Briton glanced to his side. His face had turned
bright crimson and the veins pulsating at his temples
threatened to burst. "Bloody...well...am," he
whispered between pants.

Running side by side, the two men reached the crest and the city of Cyangugu appeared a quarter mile away. Bradfordson groaned. "I was hoping we'd...be there..." he gasped.

"We're close now," Walters said.

"...or...at least...there'd be a...trolley!" Bradfordson puffed.

A good hundred yards ahead of them now, Walters saw Collier glance over his shoulder, then slow to a walk. He turned and walked back to meet Ukewere.

Walters had to decrease his pace again to keep from leaving Bradfordson behind as they neared their leader. Then suddenly the Briton had had enough, and he stopped in his tracks, bending over at the waist with his hands on his knees.

"Stand up," Walters ordered. "Give your lungs some room to expand."

Bradfordson struggled to an upright position, looking for all the world as if a heart attack was imminent.

Walters had to suppress the chuckle of satisfaction that threatened to burst from his chest. The Briton couldn't be more than thirty-five years old, tops. Taking Bradfordson's elbow, the merc led him forward.

Ukewere was even more pleased than Walters to see Bradfordson's condition. Unlike Walters, however, he made no attempt to hide it. "Too much beer," the African said happily as he and Bolan strode up to meet them.

Bradfordson nodded his agreement. "And too little squash, I'm afraid," he added as his breathing returned to normal.

Walters saw Collier eyeing the man carefully. He suspected that his fellow American had used the run for more than just a way to get into Cyangugu. Collier now knew just what kind of physical condition all three of them were in, knew what he could expect if that conditioning was put to the test. Which confirmed another suspicion Tater Walters had about John Collier.

The man wasn't just big, strong, tough and good with a gun. He was smart.

"We'll keep the pace down the rest of the way in," Bolan said. "As soon as we can, we'll pick up some wheels." He turned and broke into an easy jog. Ukewere followed, and with a quiet moan, Bradfordson fell in behind.

Still bringing up the rear, Walters watched Collier and Ukewere running side by side. What a contrast, he thought. And the differences weren't just physical. Collier, he could tell, was a man with strong moral convictions, an almost Old West code of right and wrong, and the guts to live up to his beliefs.

His head a good two feet below that of Collier's as they ran, Sal Ukewere was almost the direct opposite. Walters had known the man for almost ten years. He was a self-centered opportunist who practiced the most vile "situational ethics." He was angry at the world and never missed an opportunity to cut a taller man down to his size.

Reaching a row of run-down shacks at the edge of the city, Collier suddenly stopped, then moved off the road toward the houses. At first Walters thought the big man was stepping out of the way to let yet another group of Hutus pass.

Then the merc saw the blue-and-tan Isuzu Trooper coming up the road a quarter mile in front of them.

Bolan hurried to the houses, disappearing between two of the crumbling structures. Walters grabbed Ukewere and Bradfordson by the arms and hurried them the same way.

"What's wrong?" Bradfordson panted.

Walters nodded up the road. "Maybe you hadn't noticed," he said, "but we're the only white faces for about eight hundred miles. The refugees may be too tired to pay any attention, but whoever's driving the Trooper won't be."

Shoving the two men between the shacks, Walters circled past them to Bolan. He followed the big man back to the corner of the house and peered around to the road.

The Trooper turned down the side street on the other side of the houses.

Bolan moved around to the front, Walters, Ukewere and Bradfordson at his heels. Staying close to the wall, the big man dropped to one knee when he reached the corner.

Walters hurried up behind him, stretching his neck past the edge and following Bolan's gaze. A block and a half down the street, the Trooper had stopped. The doors of the vehicle opened and three Tutsis dressed in government army uniforms got out. They all carried Belgian assault rifles, and as Walters and Bolan watched, one of them brought the buttstock around in an arc and smashed it into the face of a passing Hutu.

The white-haired merc glanced to his side and saw his companion's eyes narrow. He didn't have to be told what they were about to do next.

5

From his vantage point between the two shanties, the Executioner watched the Isuzu Trooper turn the corner before disappearing on the other side of the house. He moved quickly into the packed dirt that made up the front yard, then sprinted to the next corner, Walters to his rear.

The Trooper came to a halt in front of a one-story frame house in slightly better shape than the other structures on the street. Except for a desperate need for new paint, the house looked livable.

The Tutsi soldiers who got out of the Trooper carried FALs, and they conversed excitedly as they walked up the sidewalk toward the front door. A lone Hutu chose that moment to cross the grass, and one of the soldiers—a lean giant close to seven feet tall—paused long enough to strike him across the face with the stock of his rifle.

The Executioner had seen the haggard Hutu making his way toward the road. The man had the same dead eyes Bolan had seen on the other Hutus trying to escape the slaughter. Now his face remained expressionless as he tumbled to the ground in front of the house—but the numb eyes closed.

Bolan fought the urge to sprint across the street after the soldier who had struck the defenseless Hutu. The laughter of the other Tutsis made it even harder. Taking a deep breath, the warrior reminded himself that he couldn't save every man, woman and child individually. But somewhere down the line in his search for Dusty Morrison and the other performers, an opportunity might arise for him to strike a blow at the enemy that would help the victims collectively.

And if that opportunity presented itself, the Executioner swore he would make good use of it.

Bolan watched the Tutsi soldiers mount the steps to the porch. Part of the problem was figuring out just who the enemy was in Rwanda. The fighting between the two tribes, the massacres, the near genocide, had been going on for centuries. Every few years the Hutus and Tutsis traded sides as oppressed and oppressor, and whoever had the guns at the moment did their best to wipe out the other tribe. Yet Bolan couldn't believe that the majority of both tribes would be no different than any other people in the world: They would be content to "live and let live" if the terrorist elements of both peoples could be persuaded to stop the madness and revenge.

He continued to watch as the tallest of the soldiers ripped open the door and led the others into the house. As things stood now, the Tutsis were in power, and killing all the Hutus they could round up. When the Hutus took over sometime in the future, history assured the Executioner that their leaders would repeat the same atrocities by slaughtering Tutsis.

Bolan turned to Walters. "Could you make out any of what they said?"

The older man shook his head. "Too far away." He paused. "How we gonna get across the street?"

The warrior almost smiled. Walters knew exactly what he had planned. The white-haired merc was proving to be more than an adequate running mate. Regardless of his age, he was a damn fine soldier, and was almost reading the Executioner's mind.

"Give it another few seconds," Bolan said. "Then we'll cross low and take up position behind the Trooper."

Walters nodded. "And them?" he asked, meaning Ukewere and Bradfordson.

Bolan hesitated. Neither man would be much help in what he had planned, but he needed to keep an eye on them. He didn't think Ukewere would run on him—at least until the man got his money—but he couldn't be sure.

Bradfordson was a wild card, as well. For a while the British playboy had appeared to be getting his jollies playing adventurer, but the long run from the plane had killed some of his enthusiasm. If he got away from them now, he might go to the authorities.

Bolan took a final glance at both the African and the Briton. "Bring them with you," he told Walters, then turned back to the house across the street.

The Executioner led the way across the pit-filled road on all fours, scrambling to a squatting position with his eyes just over the Trooper's front window.

The Tutsis had disappeared inside the house, and the sounds of a scuffle echoed out the front door.

Walters moved in next to Bolan and peered through the car's back window. Ukewere and Bradfordson fell to sitting positions on the merc's other side. "Any idea who lives here?" the warrior whispered.

The merc shook his head, then almost immediately said, "Oh, shit."

Bolan looked back at the house. Two of the soldiers were dragging a bruised and bleeding man in his early thirties down the steps toward the Trooper.

The Executioner drew the revolver from under his arm.

"That's James Nyungwe," Walters said under his breath. "Hutu rabble-rouser. Half patriot, half terrorist, and not long for this world, the way it looks."

A high-pitched scream came from inside the house, followed by gruff laughter. On the other side of the car Nyungwe cried out with a mixture of anger, hatred and frustration.

Walters and Bolan both dropped lower as the Tutsis dragged their prisoner to the Trooper. The merc turned to face the Executioner as he drew both of the .45s from his belt. "That scream would be Nyungwe's wife," he whispered. "She's even more famous than he is. Masai, from Kenya. Used to be a fashion model in Europe, and one good-lookin' lady."

Bolan had no doubt now what her scream meant. He listened as the back door of the Trooper opened and Nyungwe was thrown inside. A brief but heated argument followed. Even though he couldn't understand the language, Bolan knew what it was about.

One soldier was already busy with Nyungwe's wife. Both these men wanted to be second.

A moment later the angry voices stopped, and footsteps hurried away from the vehicle.

Bolan waited until he heard the front door of the house open and close again, gave it a count of ten, then rose and extended the .44 Magnum revolver through the open driver's-side window. The barrel stabbed into the cheek of a man sitting on the other side of the vehicle. "Don't move," the Executioner growled.

The soldier's eyes opened wide in horror. Whether he could understand English, Bolan didn't know. But he definitely got the gist of what the Executioner had said.

Walters opened the back-seat door, slid in next to Nyungwe and aimed the barrels of both Government Model pistols over the seat.

Bolan pulled his arm back out of the window. "Get in the front seat and get this thing running," he told Walters, then turned to Ukewere and Bradfordson.

"You two get in and be ready to move out."

Walters got back out of the Trooper but glanced in again at Nyungwe. "You want the cuffs to stay on?" he asked Bolan.

"You said half terrorist, didn't you?"

The merc nodded.

Bolan studied the older man's face. Tater Walters was proving his professionalism at every turn, and the

Executioner had grown to value his opinions and insight. Walters had also been in Rwanda a long time and knew Nyungwe by reputation, if not personally.

"You trust him?" Bolan asked.

"Hell no."

"Then there's your answer."

Walters exited the backseat and moved behind the wheel. Bradfordson circled the car to take the shotgun seat, and Ukewere slid in the back next to Nyungwe.

As he sprinted across the packed dirt toward the front door of the house, the Executioner heard Nyungwe's wife scream again.

Three steps led to the small porch in front of the door.

The rotted wood of the first two cracked like rifle shots as Bolan's feet hit them. The third collapsed completely under his weight.

The warrior felt the sharp slivers of wood shred through his sock as his calf plummeted down through the hole. He reached out, catching his balance on the edge of the porch, and jerked his foot free. Leaping up the steps, he burst through the open door into a small living area.

What little furniture the house contained had been covered with ragged white sheets. Cardboard boxes, their flaps taped to conceal the contents, had been stacked against the wall.

Another scream, from the rear of the house, was cut off suddenly and replaced by a low, guttural laugh.

With the .44 Magnum revolver leading the way, Bolan followed the sound down a short hallway past the open door to a bathroom, dipping a shoulder as he turned into the bedroom. Before him, he saw a bare mattress on the floor against the wall. On her back, her long lean legs bare and kicking the air, lay a black woman. Ocher-dyed mud held her hair in place in the tradition of the Masai, and enormous gold earrings hung from her ears.

On top of her, his knees pinning her shoulders to the mattress while his hands fought to catch her flailing wrists, was one of the Tutsi soldiers Bolan had seen enter the house. The other, a short and pudgy man by Tutsi standards, wore an OD soda-jerk cap and stood to one side of the mattress. He had already unbuckled his belt and unzipped his pants.

The shorter man looked up in surprise as the Executioner burst into the room. His right hand grabbed at the holstered revolver at his side, but as his fingers released his trousers the weight of the weapon jerked them down to his knees.

The Tutsi's hand groped air where the gun had been a moment before.

Bolan raised the S&W, double-actioning a quick pair of Magnum rounds that threatened to deafen everyone in the room. The hollowpoints blew through the sternum of the would-be rapist and took half of his spine with them as they exited his back.

The Executioner turned toward the mattress, where the other man had released the woman's wrists. The Tutsi had unsnapped the flap holster on his belt and gotten a grip on his pistol, but as he brought the weapon into play, the woman reached up and slapped at his hand.

The barrel of the weapon moved no more than an inch. But an inch for the barrel translated into a good six feet as the round crossed the room to sail harmlessly by the Executioner and into the wall.

Bolan squeezed the trigger again and the Smith jumped in his hand. Another 240-grain hollow point exploded from the revolver and drilled into the Tutsi's left lung, blood flying from both his chest and back. The force of the round threw the man against the wall, where he hung for a moment before slowly sinking to the floor.

The woman on the mattress looked up at the Executioner as she pulled her short skirt down around her shapely thighs. Bolan broke the revolver open, dumped the remaining rounds into the side pocket of his jacket and dropped a speed-loader into the cylinder.

The woman rose to her feet, her expression a mixture of fear, relief and curiosity. She spoke in Kinyarwanda, and when Bolan shook his head, switched to French. "Who are you?" she asked.

The Executioner answered in the same language. "The guy you're leaving with. Unless you want to wait around for more of these guys to show up."

The woman faced him now. Her legs apart, hands on her hips, she stared defiantly up into his eyes. "Is Jim with you?" she demanded. "James Nyungwe. I'm not going with you unless my husband's all right."

"He's in the car with a friend of mine," Bolan said. "Come on." He took the woman's arm, leading her out of the room, down the hall and out the door.

They had made it to the front porch when the second Isuzu Trooper squealed into the front yard.

The barrel of an assault rifle stabbed out the passenger's-side window, aimed at the vehicle where Walters, Ukewere, Bradfordson and Nyungwe sat. Bolan could see two more uniformed men in the backseat of the approaching vehicle.

A burst of automatic rifle fire rang out, and Bolan heard a moan from inside Walters's vehicle. Raising the S&W to eye level, he lined up the sights.

The .44 Magnum revolver exploded once, and the Tutsi driving the second Trooper slumped forward over the wheel. Bolan aimed through the gap between the man's back and the seat, double-actioning another round that sent the assault rifle falling from the other side of the Trooper to the ground.

A volley of rounds burst from the backseat of the vehicle, peppering the front porch. The Executioner grabbed the woman, pulling her to the ground and rolling over her. As he fell, he heard the distinct sound of .45 fire from Walters's Government Models.

The S&W jumped in Bolan's hand again as he hit the ground on top of Nyungwe's wife. He had snapped the round more as cover than defense, and it struck the post behind the back seat of the Trooper. Taking his time now, Bolan centered the red-ramp front site between the white outline on the rear notch and squeezed once more.

As the hammer traveled back, he heard another double tap of .45s explode from Walters's position. The .45ACPs and .44 Magnum rounds teamed up, taking out both of the Tutsis in the backseat of the Trooper. As the trio of roars died down, the Executioner heard a car door open as he leaped to his feet, jerking the woman up with him. The big .44 revolver still at the ready, he looked across the yard to see the rear door of the first Isuzu standing open.

Twenty yards beyond the vehicle, Sal Ukewere's legs were propelling him down the street as fast as they could.

Bolan pulled the woman down the steps to the yard and across the dirt toward the Trooper. Walters was leaning in the open door, and as Bolan and Mrs. Nyungwe approached, the merc turned and shook his head.

The warrior looked past the white-haired man to where James Nyungwe sat, his hands cuffed behind his back, staring blindly ahead. The bullet had entered just below the man's nose.

Those dead eyes were all that was left of his face.

DUSTY MORRISON MOVED quietly around a curve in the narrow jungle trail, as he led his companions through the Rugege Forest.

The aging Western star stepped over a mud puddle, shoved a branch in front of him and stepped past it. Then, ever so carefully, he eased the branch back into place, dropping both hands to the stag grips of the twin Colt Peacemaker guns on his hips. He had reloaded the half-empty single-action revolvers before they left their violated sanctuary, and both carried five rounds of bird shot with the hammers resting on an empty chamber for safety. That left only four rounds in the loops of the Buscadero rig.

Fourteen shots total, if he had to shoot. But the bird shot was weak and would have little effect on a man unless fired almost point-blank.

Behind him, the Western star heard a loud crack as a branch snapped under someone's foot. Turning, he saw Spaak round the curve. The man glared at him briefly, then averted his eyes as he jumped over the puddle.

The cowboy caught his breath. He and Spaak had engaged in a short argument right after the Tutsi soldiers' departure from the underground house. Morrison had insisted that they quickly pack what they could carry and get out of there before the men returned. Spaak had argued that they were safer staying put, that the soldiers probably wouldn't return, and if they did, they would never find the door.

Streak's insistence that the men had heard the toilet flush, and Morrison's argument that the men were probably smart enough to know that toilets didn't grow on trees in the middle of the Rugege Forest, hadn't seemed to matter to Spaak. He'd also chosen to ignore the fact that they'd said they were bringing a metal detector back with them.

The disagreement had ended when Morrison told the others that he was leaving, and that anyone who wanted to come was welcome. Neither LeFevre nor

Streak had hesitated, and Dusty Morrison had thereby been elected leader of the group, a position Hubert Spaak wanted, if for no other reason than to promote himself in LeFevre's eyes.

Morrison waited as Spaak pushed past the outstretched branch and stopped next to him, turning his back. The egotistical horse's ass wasn't going to forgive him. But maybe it wasn't entirely the kid's fault. The Western star suspected the ability to forgive wasn't in the young man's psychological makeup any more than any number of other normal human virtues.

LeFevre and Streak appeared around the curve and stopped in front of the puddle as if it were the size of the Atlantic. Then Streak turned around and retreated several steps before turning back again. With a determined look on his face, he sprinted forward and jumped.

The makeup artist's feet hit the puddle three-fourths of the way across, slipped out from under him and sent him splashing to his back in a flurry of flying mud and dirty water.

The actress screamed as mud splattered over her. Cursing under her breath, she wiped it from her eyes, then trudged through the puddle to help Streak to his feet.

Morrison waited until they'd joined him and Spaak, then whispered, "Listen, we've got to be more quiet. We can't be over a hundred yards from the house, and when they come back—"

As if to finish the sentence for him, the sound of someone nearby drifted through the trees from the direction of the underground house.

The four escapees froze in their tracks. Morrison's right hand fell involuntarily to the Colts, and he turned to the makeup artist. "Listen close, Streak," he said so low it was almost inaudible. "Can you tell what they're saying?"

Streak cocked an ear. The Western star held his breath as he waited. He had done his best to restore the campfire that had camouflaged the door, replacing the ashes and charred pieces of wood. But he had no idea how they had lain before. Rukanwe had built the fire after they were already inside the house, and it was anybody's guess what the remains had looked like before the trapdoor disrupted them.

If one of the men who had been there earlier noticed the change—and Morrison couldn't see how anyone but a complete fool could miss it—the Tutsi troops would find the underground house without needing the metal detector. When that happened, they'd learn that the actors had vacated the premises and start to search the forest.

The aging actor knew they couldn't afford to make any noise, but they couldn't afford to stay close to the house, either. They had to keep moving, get as far away from the vicinity as possible.

Morrison looked at LeFevre, Streak and Spaak. Could they walk without alerting the men searching the clearing? So far they'd made more noise than the elephants Dusty knew were roaming the Rugege Forest.

Turning to the makeup artist again, Morrison whispered in his ear. "Can you make anything out?"

Streak could barely speak. "They... haven't found the door yet," he murmured, his voice trembling. "But they... they know who we are."

Morrison nodded. Belgians were at the top of the hit list of both Hutu and Tutsi, and the acting troupe's country of origin was well-known. People would have been searching for them from the beginning. And now they'd been found—at least almost.

Moving silently, his eyes searching the ground before his boots set down, Morrison moved from Streak to where LeFevre and Spaak now stood. "We've got to go," he said. "But we have to go slow. Keep your eyes on the ground, and don't step on anything that might make noise." He paused, feeling his heart hammer against his chest, then added, "Follow me."

With that, he set off at a snail's pace, leading his companions into the jungle.

BOLAN LOOKED UP in time to see Sal Ukewere duck out of sight between two houses on the other side of the street. Turning back, he saw that Mrs. Nyungwe, still behind him, hadn't yet seen her husband. Shifting to block her view of the backseat, the Executioner looked at Bradfordson. "We can't stay here," he said. "More troops may be on the way. Art, take Mrs. Nyungwe and get in the other Trooper."

The woman shook her head violently back and forth. "I want to ride with my husband," she said, trying to edge around Bolan. "Jim . . . Jimmy . . ."

The Executioner shoved her away. "Tater, help Art get her loaded, then come back and drive this vehicle. Both of you meet me a mile south of here."

"When?" Walters asked.

Bolan shrugged. "As soon as I catch Sal." He turned and sprinted down the street, cutting between the same two shacks where Ukewere had disappeared. A small chicken house sat at the rear of the property, the birds eaten long ago by their starving owners. Bolan moved to the coop, stepped over the short fence and checked inside. Empty.

An open field, roughly a quarter-mile square, lay directly behind the houses at the edge of Cyangugu. In the distance the warrior saw what appeared to be a coffee plantation. He moved from the chicken house to the edge of the field, his eyes scanning the ground for tracks.

He found them. More than he wanted. Hundreds if not thousands of feet had trampled the grass and weeds recently. Hutus fleeing to the Rwanda-Zaire border had obviously cut across the field.

Bolan turned back to the row of dilapidated houses behind him. Unless Ukewere had ducked inside the back door of one of the crumbling structures, the little man was crouched somewhere in the tall grass of the field. The Executioner had paid close attention as Ukewere jogged from the landing strip into town, and been surprised that the man had run as well as he had.

But Ukewere wasn't fast enough to have crossed the entire field before Bolan arrived at the scene, and except for the houses, there was nowhere else to hide.

The Executioner took a final glance up and down the rear of the shacks. Unless Ukewere knew someone who lived in one of the structures—an unlikely possibility—he would have chosen the field.

Breaking into a slow jog, Bolan started across the grass. His keen eyes swept back and forth across the field in front of him, zeroing in on anything that looked out of place. He thought for a moment that he'd found Ukewere beneath a bush, but the gaudy swatch of material he'd spotted proved to be nothing more than a discarded skirt someone had abandoned on the way to the border.

Bolan reached the far edge of the field and started back, jogging a zigzag path this time. Somewhere in the field, Ukewere was lying low, and even though the warrior hadn't spotted him, Ukewere had more than likely seen him by now.

Reaching the center of the field, Bolan stopped. He turned a full 360-degree circle, but still saw nothing. For a moment he considered leaving Ukewere and continuing his search for Morrison without the African. He had Walters, who knew Rwanda almost as well as Ukewere. But the operative word was "almost," and the Executioner suspected that certain avenues of information would be closed to the white man simply because of the color of his skin.

No. He still needed Sal Ukewere.

The Executioner cupped his hands over his mouth. "Sal!" he shouted. "Sal, I know you're out here somewhere, and sooner or later I'm going to find you! I know it, and you know it. So you can come out now, or we can waste a lot of time while I look for you. That will also give more Tutsis a chance to get here. But one way or the other, Sal, I'm not leaving without you!"

Bolan dropped his hands to his sides and waited.

Thirty seconds later he saw a clump of grass move fifty yards to his right. Sal Ukewere rose to his feet and started slowly forward. The man's clothes and hair were covered with dried grass. Mud stained his shirt and trousers. As he neared, his expression of guilt changed to one of anger, and Bolan saw the same deep-seated hatred he'd seen before.

Ten yards away, Ukewere stopped. "If I had a gun, I'd have killed you," he snarled.

Bolan turned and started back across the field. "Let's go, Sal. The others are waiting on us."

BOTH TUTSI ARMY Isuzu Troopers were waiting by the time Bolan and Ukewere arrived at the remains of what had once been a small post office. Sometime during the war that never really stopped in Rwanda, a bomb—maybe Tutsi, maybe Hutu—had taken its toll on the building. Little but the foundation, a couple of walls and one row of post office boxes remained.

The Troopers were waiting across the street, their engines running. Walters sat behind the wheel of the nearer vehicle. Mrs. Nyungwe had taken the back seat.

She stared blankly at the windshield, dried tears on her face.

Walters got out of the vehicle and walked toward Bolan and Ukewere as they approached. "She saw him," he said without preamble. "Jumped out as soon as we parked. I couldn't stop her."

The warrior nodded. Mrs. Nyungwe had been bound to find out that her husband was dead, but he would have liked to have broken the news more gently. Seeing James Nyungwe's semifaceless corpse wasn't the way to do it.

But that was the way things went down sometimes in war, and there was nothing the Executioner could do to change that fact.

Walking to the Trooper, Bolan got in next to the woman. "I'm sorry," he said simply. There was nothing else he could say.

She nodded, her eyes closed.

"What's your name?" Bolan asked.

The Masai woman's eyes opened, and she forced a thin smile. "You couldn't pronounce it if I told you," she said. "To Westerners, I go by Janet. Janet Nyungwe."

"Janet it is, then." Bolan paused. "I'm Collier." He glanced up the street. "We've got to get out of here before more of the Tutsi troops show up."

The woman nodded.

The Executioner leaned forward to speak to Walters, who had returned to the wheel of the Trooper. "Tater, I'm sending Bradfordson over to ride with you. I'll take Sal with me. You know any place we can lie low until this has died down a little?''

Walters's eyebrows lowered in thought. "Not really. Cyangugu isn't my usual stomping grounds.''

Janet spoke next to Bolan. "I have a friend," she said. "They have a plantation near here. It may not be safe, but it will be better than anywhere else I can think of.''

"Then it'll have to do," Bolan said. "Tater, Janet will give you the directions. You lead the way." He got out of the backseat, hurried to the other Trooper, slid behind the wheel and sent Bradfordson back to Walters. Ukewere got in without a word. A few seconds later both vehicles pulled out.

Bolan followed Walters as Janet directed them through the neighborhood of crumbling shacks and huts. Ten minutes later they left Cyangugu for the road that eventually led to Butare.

"Where are we going?" Ukewere demanded.

"Someplace where we can stay out of sight for a while," Bolan informed him.

The warrior began to feel uneasy as they passed several vehicles going the opposite way. Even though the Troopers were unmarked, the drivers looked nervously through the windows as they passed, obviously recognizing the vehicles as belonging to the Tutsi-controlled government. That meant that any Tutsi soldiers they encountered would recognize the twin Troopers, as well.

Janet directed them past a tea-processing plant, and fields of cotton. The Troopers maneuvered up and over several long rolling hills, then Walters's vehicle slowed and turned onto a gravel drive.

Bolan followed the white-haired merc over the bumpy path to a large colonial-style house a hundred yards off the road. They pulled onto a circular drive and parked near the front door.

Walters and Janet Nyungwe got out of the lead Trooper, Bolan joining them on the way to the front porch. Hurrying up the steps, he rammed a huge brass knocker against the wood several times.

Moments later the door swung open and another startlingly beautiful black woman in her midtwenties stood in the opening in a form-fitting sarong. Gold hoop earrings hung from her earlobes. Her hair was cropped close to her head, leaving only a short layer of black curls.

She smiled at Janet, then her eyes moved to Bolan. When they got to Tater Walters, her mouth suddenly dropped open in shock.

"Well, I'll be damned," Walters muttered, his own lower lip falling.

Then the beautiful young woman was in his arms.

"You know each other?" Janet asked in surprise, though Walters and the woman were too engrossed in each other to hear.

Behind him, the Executioner heard Ukewere and Bradfordson mounting the steps. Walters and the young woman forced themselves to arm's length and stared into each other's eyes.

Ukewere stopped in his tracks. "I know you," the man said. "You're—"

Walters's hand snaked out to grab the little man's throat. The aging mercenary shook his head slightly and glowered at Ukewere.

The woman cleared her throat. "Please come inside," she said. Still holding Walters's hand, she turned and led them into the house.

The Executioner raised a questioning eyebrow at Janet, who shook her head and shrugged. They moved through an elaborate living room decorated in Western style but featuring African art, then passed by a fully equipped gym. Bolan saw muscle-building machines, a treadmill, two stationary bikes and a small trampoline.

Emerging into a less formal sitting room, the woman of the house dropped gracefully into a carved Victorian love seat. She motioned for the others to sit, as well.

Walters nervously cleared his throat. "Waseme," he said, "this is John Collier." He nodded toward Bolan, then said, "And Art Bradfordson. Guys, this is Waseme . . . Duke." He paused. "You already know Janet and Ukewere. Where's Godfrey, Waseme?"

The woman smiled at Bolan. "Godfrey is my husband, Mr. Collier."

She turned back to Walters. "He's in the fields, Tater. So many of our workers have fled to the border that he is helping pick the cotton himself." She turned to Janet. "Where is James?"

Janet Nyungwe burst into tears as an answer.

Waseme Duke rose and hurried across the room, taking a seat on the couch next to the woman and throwing both arms around her. "Oh...no," she said as she hugged her friend.

Walters stood suddenly. "Waseme, we ran into a little trouble in Cyangugu. I know it's a lot to ask with everything that's going on, but we need a place to lie low. Regroup. We also need to trade you out of some wheels the government won't recognize. And we need some information that you may or may not have."

Waseme smiled slightly. "Tater, was there ever a time when you were *not* in some kind of trouble?"

Walters chuckled, his gaze softening as he stared at the woman. Bolan didn't know the story, but the feelings the white-haired merc had for Waseme were obvious.

Waseme patted Janet on the shoulder and stood. "Perhaps you should move your cars into the barn where they will not be seen from the road."

Then, looking at Janet, Bradfordson and Ukewere, she said, "We have plenty of room for as long as you like. I'll have baths run for you and show you to your rooms."

"Thanks, Waseme," Walters said.

"When have I ever said no to you, Tater?" the woman asked, looking down as she smoothed her sarong with both hands.

"Waseme, I—I—" Walters stammered.

The woman looked him squarely in the eye. "You don't have to answer that."

The Executioner had watched the looks that passed between Tater Walters and Waseme Duke. They were close friends—at least close friends—and Bolan suspected they had to have once been much more.

Walters led Bolan back through the house and out to the driveway. They drove the Troopers around the side of the house and through an open barn door.

"I might as well tell you and get it over with," Walters said as they walked back toward the house. "You noticed that Waseme and I know each other pretty well?"

"Well, I'm not blind."

Walters face suddenly fell. "We used to be engaged."

Bolan didn't answer.

"Yeah, yeah, I know," the white-haired mercenary said. "I'm old enough to be her father." He paused. "Okay, *grand*father."

The Executioner shrugged. "I didn't say anything."

"Well, you couldn't help thinking it. Lord knows, *I* thought about it enough." He led the way back up the front steps, then stopped and turned. "She used to live in Kigali. She was a prostitute." He paused. "That's why a little street vermin like Ukewere knows her. What do you think of that, Collier?"

"I think it's none of my business," the Executioner replied.

Walters broke eye contact again and looked up at the sky. "I should have married her," he said, more to himself than to Bolan. "Before she met Godfrey."

"Why didn't you?"

The aging warrior looked back at Bolan. "I wasn't ready to settle down yet," he said with a straight face, then turned and walked back into the house.

6

The hot water stinging his skin washed the dirt of two days from the Executioner, revitalizing both his body and spirit. Twisting the knob, he opened the translucent glass door, reached out of the shower and jerked a large bath towel from the rack on the wall.

As he dried himself, Bolan assessed the situation as it stood. He didn't really know if he was any closer to finding Dusty Morrison and the Belgians than he had been when he stepped off the plane in Kigali. He was following the only lead he had, and for all he knew, it could stop any time at a dead end.

The Executioner stepped out of the shower and dried his hair with another towel, then walked naked into the bedroom he'd been assigned in the huge cotton-plantation house. One of the servants had left a fresh white shirt and khaki slacks on the bed that Bolan suspected belonged to Godfrey Duke. He slipped into the slacks.

No, he couldn't be sure that Zaid Karsimbi would know where Big Billy Rukanwe was, or if Rukanwe would know where the actors were. And according to Ukewere, Karsimbi was a paranoid local hood, which

meant there would be certain complications to over-
come before he got to the man.

All of which would take time—time during which
both Hutu and Tutsi would be hunting down, and
killing, all the Belgians they could find.

Bolan zipped up the slacks and began threading his
belt through the loops. The cuffs of the khakis hit him
above the ankles, and a quick glance at the shirt still
folded on the bed told him it wouldn't fit any better.

Well, he might not be invited to pose for *Gentlemen's Quarterly* in Godfrey Duke's clothes, but at
least the pants fit in the waist, and he suspected he'd
be able to get the shirt buttoned.

Reaching under the pillow, Bolan produced the
Smith & Wesson 629 and Browning Hi-Power. He had
given both weapons only a cursory glance as to function before being pressed into battle. The Smith had
stood up under fire, which was the true test of a firearm. But he wanted to check it more thoroughly to
make sure it would perform over the long haul. And
the Browning Hi-Power had yet to throw a round.

Thumbing the Smith & Wesson's cylinder latch,
Bolan dumped the rounds on the bed. He worked the
ejector rod several times to make sure it moved
smoothly, then spun the cylinder. The latch at the
bottom of the frame seemed to function well, and
when he swung the wheel back into the gun and
cocked the trigger, the cylinder locked tightly. His
thumb on the hammer spur, the Executioner eased the
hammer back down. Reloading the weapon, he
slipped it into the shoulder rig.

The warrior picked up the Browning, dumped the 13-round 9 mm magazine and worked the slide to flip the round from the chamber. His mind drifted to Art Bradfordson. It was time to get rid of the Englishman before he got hurt. The Briton had the heart of an adventurer, but he lacked the skills to back up that heart. He was a nice guy, and he deserved to have the chance to go on being a nice guy—a chance he wasn't likely to get if he hung around with the Executioner much longer.

Locking the Hi-Power's slide back, Bolan pushed the latch out of the weapon and separated the frame from the slide. He pulled out the barrel, recoil spring and guide, and inspected each piece carefully as his mind turned to Janet Nyungwe. Walters and Bradfordson had taken her husband's body to a small meadow nearby, where they would bury him. Bolan had suggested it, and the man's widow hadn't objected.

In war-torn Rwanda, funeral services, like so many other things most people took for granted, became an extravagance.

Satisfied that the Browning would perform when called upon, Bolan assembled and loaded the weapon. He shoved it into the holster, then looped the leather through his belt.

He hadn't met Godfrey Duke yet, but there was a chance he'd know Karsimbi. The local hood had legitimate business interests in the area, and if he and Duke were acquainted, Duke might be able to provide an introduction. If not, they'd have to get inside to see the man however they could. Which would probably mean more shooting.

Bolan looked down at both the Smith & Wesson and the Browning. That meant they'd need more firepower than the pistols he and Walters were carrying.

A soft knock outside the bedroom tore the Executioner from his thoughts.

He stood and moved to the door, his hand close to the Hi-Power. "Yes?" he said, standing to one side of the frame.

"It's me," Walters said.

Bolan reached for the knob. The door swung open and Walters entered. The merc wore a pair of khakis identical to Bolan's, but they were too long, breaking over the tops of his hiking boots. Walters's white shirt was a twin of Bolan's, as well, but slightly too large.

The older man glanced at Bolan's bare chest as he stepped into the room. "Looks like you've seen a little action over the years," he said. "Caught a bullet or two."

"One or two," he agreed.

Walters stopped in the middle of the room as the Executioner closed the door again. "Thought so," he said. "'Course it's a little hard to see under all the knife-wound scars."

Bolan grabbed the shirt off the bed and shrugged into it. "Where are Art and Sal?" he asked.

"Asleep," Walters said. "Godfrey's back."

"You know him?"

Walters shook his head. "Never met him. Just heard him come in."

"What does he know about Waseme's past?"

"Only what he needs to know," Walters replied. "She's going to tell him I'm an old friend from the Kigali days. He thinks she worked at a vegetable stand in the market."

The Executioner finished buttoning his shirt, leaving the top two open to compensate for the tight fit in the shoulders. "How you going to keep Ukewere quiet?" he asked as he donned the shoulder harness.

Walters shrugged. "Sal's a major-league asshole sometimes. But I've already explained in lurid detail what will happen to him if he opens his mouth. I think I made my point." He paused. "She's a good woman, John," he said. "She's human like all of us, so she's made some mistakes in her life. But I won't let anybody destroy what she's got now."

The Executioner didn't bother answering as he covered his weapons with his sport coat.

"Anyway," the white-haired merc went on, "Godfrey's downstairs waiting on us."

Bolan followed Walters down the stairs to the same sitting room where they'd spoken with Waseme earlier.

A middle-aged man of medium height and build with a waxed handlebar mustache sat on the love seat. He rose and extended his hand as Walters and Bolan entered the room. The man wore a pair of khakis and a white shirt, and Bolan suspected now that this had to be Godfrey Duke's personal plantation "uniform."

Duke's clothes were covered with dirt and small fluffs of cotton.

"Mr. Collier," Duke said in British-accented English. "I am Godfrey Duke." He smiled to show two rows of tiny white teeth.

Waseme glided into the room and placed a silver tea set on the coffee table.

"Sit down, my dear," Duke said.

She moved in front of the love seat and they sat down together. Bolan and Walters dropped into chairs across from them.

"I understand you gentlemen are in some sort of trouble," Duke said. Without waiting for an answer, he added, "Understandable, considering everything." He looked down at the silver service in front of him. "We shall dispense with more formalities under the circumstances." Pouring tea into an ornately painted china cup, he lifted the saucer beneath it and handed it to Bolan. "Sugar or cream?"

Bolan shook his head.

Still holding the silver pitcher, Duke looked up and smiled. "So. How can I help you?"

"Do you know Big Billy Rukanwe?" Bolan asked.

Duke poured more tea and handed the cup and saucer to Walters. "No, Mr. Collier, I regret to say, I do not."

Bolan took a sip of the tea. "How about Zaid Karsimbi?"

Duke stiffened slightly, then poured tea for himself and his wife. "I have met him," he said. "But we are certainly not friends."

"Enemies?"

"No, no," Duke said. "I suppose we would nod should we encounter each other on the street." He coughed affectedly, sounding for all he was worth like the stuffy, stereotypical English gentleman. "Waseme and I attended a fund-raiser at his home once, but I want to stress to you, Mr. Collier, I do not befriend men like Zaid Karsimbi."

Bolan crossed his legs and leaned forward slightly. "I understand his house is protected."

Duke laughed. "That is perhaps the understatement of the century, Mr. Collier. A high wall runs around his property, and guards stand watch in little concrete towers. Waseme and I were forced to pass through a metal detector before entering his house." He shook his head. "The man is a true paranoid."

The Executioner uncrossed his legs. "Do you know him well enough to set up an appointment where I could talk to him?" he asked. He set his teacup on an end table next to his chair.

Duke stood, walked across the room to a shelf-lined wall and lifted a yellow-and-white calabash pipe from its rack. He stuffed it hastily with tobacco from a jar next to the rack, then returned to his seat. "I could try," he said. "But may I ask why you would wish to hold conference with a man of that...caliber?"

"I believe he can help us locate Big Billy."

Duke pulled a lighter from his shirt pocket and held it over the bowl of his pipe. When smoke rose toward the ceiling, he bit the stem and said around it, "Yes, I understand they are friends, although I cannot fathom

it. Rukanwe is reputed to be a good and honest man."
He looked up suddenly. "You are here to rescue the
Belgian theater players?"

Bolan nodded. The man had already figured it out,
and there was little sense denying the fact.

Duke held the pipe away from his mouth. "Are you
CIA, Mr. Collier?"

The Executioner shook his head. "It's an independent operation."

Duke looked at Walters. "And you, Mr. Walters?"

"Not anymore."

The Englishman turned to his wife and smiled.
"Dear, could you possibly bring us another pot of
tea?"

Waseme frowned. "The pot is still—"

"I believe it has grown cold, my dear," Duke insisted. "If you would, please."

"It can't be cold—"

"Please, dear."

Waseme finally took the hint, rose, lifted the silver
tray and exited the room.

Duke took several puffs on his pipe as the beautiful
woman walked down the hall out of earshot. Then he
held the calabash away from him again. "Were you
one of her customers, Mr. Walters?" he asked
abruptly.

The merc nodded. "I used to buy vegetables from
her there at the—"

Duke closed his eyes and shook his head, the
movement stopping Walters in midsentence.

"Mr. Walters, please. I know far more about my wife's past than you—or she, for that matter—suspect. Please answer my question. Were you one of her customers?"

Bolan watched the white-haired man out of the corner of his eye. Walters face betrayed the fact that he didn't know whether to lie or go with the truth. Finally he said, "I was in love with her."

Duke nodded slowly. "Yes. Yes. Then you are the one."

An uncomfortable silence fell over the room.

"Oh, dear me," Duke suddenly said. "I'm afraid I've given you the wrong impression. Perhaps I should clarify myself." He puffed twice on his pipe, then said, "Yes, I am aware that Waseme was a prostitute. No, she does not know that I possess that knowledge. And as far as you being 'the one,' I know only that there was an older man with whom she was once in love, a man who was one of her customers but treated her well, and was in love with her." He puffed again, but the pipe had gone out. "She talks in her sleep, you see," he said as he flicked the lighter once more. "But perhaps you already know that."

Walters remained tastefully silent.

As soon as the pipe was relit, Duke said, "To answer a question that I see you are both too polite to ask, yes, the whole thing does bother me somewhat. But I've come to terms with Waseme's past, and myself. I live with it, and consider myself lucky to have her as a wife."

"You are, Mr. Duke," Walters said softly. "You are."

Duke stood. "Yes...quite." Moving to a phone on an end table next to the love seat, he lifted the receiver. "Let me see if I can ring up Mr. Karsimbi," he said.

He tapped in three numbers and a moment later said, "Yes, indeed. I'd like a residential number for Mr. Zaid Karsimbi." After a short pause, he added, "Thank you," disconnected the line, then dialed the number.

Bolan and Walters waited.

"Yes, hello yourself. This is Mr. Godfrey Duke, don't you know. May I speak to Mr. Karsimbi, please?"

The warrior saw a flicker of movement to his side and looked over to see Waseme entering the room. Steam rose from the spout of the silver teapot as she returned it to the coffee table and looked at her husband.

Duke motioned for her to sit. A second later he said into the receiver, "Yes, I understand. Thank you very much." He hung up.

He turned to face Bolan and Walters. "I was told that Mr. Karsimbi was absent. But the man who informed me of such did so in a way that meant that Karsimbi was there but that I should fuck off." He glanced to his wife and said, "Pardon my language, dear."

Waseme acted as if she hadn't heard.

Bolan stood. "We've got to talk to him, anyway," he said. "I guess it'll have to be the hard way." He turned to face Duke. "Do you have any rifles?"

The Englishman smiled. "Oh my, yes. And I'll be delighted to assist you personally, as well. Did I mention I had been in Her Majesty's army?"

KARUZI HADN'T exaggerated. Zaid Karsimbi's home *was* a fortress.

Behind the wheel of Godfrey Duke's Lincoln Continental, the Executioner squinted through compact binoculars at the dusty brown concrete walls that encircled the property. He and Walters had left Bradfordson, Ukewere and Janet Nyungwe exhausted and asleep at the plantation to drive the five miles back into Cyangugu and recon Karsimbi's house.

Setting up surveillance had been no problem, as the compound was situated directly across the street from a park near downtown Cyangugu. The fighting had died down again, and several other vehicles were parked in the circular drive that ran in front of rusty swing sets, jungle gyms and a threadbare trampoline with an aluminum frame.

Several lookout posts extended above the ten-foot walls, and in them the Executioner could see armed men. Occasionally one of them left the post to patrol along the ledge that had to run on the other side of the wall.

Next to him, Bolan heard Tater Walters's soft steady breathing. A quick glance to his side showed the older man's brows deep in thought as he contemplated the same problem that was on the Executioner's mind.

Bolan shifted the binoculars to a half dozen oscillating surveillance cameras mounted on top of the walls. From the angles at which they sat, it appeared they would pick up anything that came into view within approximately ten feet of the fortress.

The Executioner dropped the binoculars to his lap. Duke had been unable to get him an appointment with Karsimbi, but there was still the chance that he could just walk up to the door and knock. Maybe he could talk his way past the guards, and gain entry to...

Bolan let the thought die in his head. No, Karsimbi was boarded up because of the outbreak of war. He wasn't taking chances. It would never work; he'd be turned away, and then the guards would be even more cautious when he attempted to enter the compound through other means.

Turning halfway around, Bolan looked at the blanket spread across the backseat. Godfrey Duke had beamed with pride when Bolan had asked about rifles. And the Englishman *did* have a nice collection— at least fifty long guns in various makes and caliber. But they were all sporting pieces.

The Winchester 94 30-30 Bolan had finally chosen was still an excellent design after well over a hundred years. Duke, the Executioner suspected, had probably used it to take his share of gazelles, warthogs and similar midsize African game. In the hands of a man who knew how to use it, the lever-action rifle also made a far better defense weapon than most people understood.

But for the blanket of cover fire the Executioner would have preferred under these circumstances, it was hardly the ideal firearm.

Walters had picked out a Weatherby Mark V Deluxe to add to his brace of .45s. The .416 Magnum rifle would take down an elephant. But it was the epitome of overkill on human targets, and the massive recoil and bolt action meant slow follow-up shots.

Still, the two rifles had been the best of the lot. And they were all the Executioner had. So he would make the most of them.

Turning back to the walls, Bolan frowned. The ten-foot barrier looked slick, with no hand- or footholds. Climbing it was out of the question. Walters was going to attract the guards' attention, and the warrior would have to come up with a way of getting over it before time ran out.

Closing his eyes, the Executioner rubbed his forehead. Other than Walters, it was a ragtag group of noncombatants he'd picked up along the way, and he not only couldn't count on them as a fighting unit, he didn't feel right about risking their lives. Godfrey Duke's service in "Her Majesty's army," as he'd put it, had turned out to be in the King's Troop, Royal Horse Brigade—the only purely ceremonial unit in the entire British army.

Unlike the Guards Division and Household Cavalry, the unit had no training in a combat environment.

"Any ideas?" Walters asked.

Before the Executioner could reply, the sound of people passing in front of the car made him open his eyes. Through the windshield he saw a Tutsi family walking across the park. A little girl of roughly four years broke away from the group and ran toward the shreds of canvas hanging from the trampoline frame.

The idea came fast and hard.

At first it seemed insane, but as the Executioner let the notion play around in his brain, adding details here and there and developing concept into conception, it began to appear workable.

Bolan felt Walters's eyes on him and glanced at the men.

"Got something?" the merc asked.

The Executioner nodded, then told him what he had in mind. "Considering the equipment and personnel we have to work with, it's the only thing I can think of," he said, then twisted the key, started the engine and threw the Lincoln into gear.

As Bolan backed out of the parking space that faced Karsimbi's compound, Walters stared out through the windshield, then suddenly chuckled. "Know what it is I like about you, Collier?" he asked.

When the Executioner made no reply, the white-haired mercenary said, "You're damn near the only guy I've ever known who's loonier than I am."

AN HOUR LATER Bolan pulled the Lincoln into the same space it had occupied during the recon phase of the mission. He lifted the communication apparatus from the seat next to him and wrapped the headset over his head, positioning the voice-activated microphone in front of his mouth. "Testing, one, two, three," he said. The voice-activated microphone keyed on. "You read me, Tater?"

"Loud and clear," Walters replied.

"How about you, Duke?" Bolan asked.

"Quite," the plantation owner added.

"Roger," Bradfordson responded.

By now Walters would be setting up on the tree-lined knoll on the other side of Karsimbi's compound. The two Englishmen were in the Ford pickup Duke used on the plantation. Both teams were awaiting his orders to go into action.

Bolan clipped the transceiver to his belt. The communication units were hardly of the quality used at Stony Man Farm. They transmitted over FM waves and had a range of only a quarter mile. Used primarily by cyclists, hikers and hunters, these particular units had been used by Godfrey Duke to establish hands-free communication with the men and women working his cotton fields.

They were short-range, but should be enough to keep in touch during what was about to go down.

The warrior raised the binoculars for one last look at the guards along the wall. He was the only one taking any risk. Walters would be far enough away that the guards wouldn't spot him during the short period of time he'd be shooting, and the two Englishmen should be "in and out" before the enemy was even aware of their presence.

The Executioner leaned over the backseat, jerked the blanket off the Winchester and laid the weapon across his lap. He checked the sling swivels to make sure they were secure, then worked the lever, chambering the first of the 30-30 softpoints, then lowered the hammer. "Tater, you set up?"

"That's affirmative. Ready when you are."

"Bradfordson and Duke?"

"Set to roll," Godfrey Duke replied.

"Then let's do it," the warrior said into the mike.

A second later Tater Walters pulled the trigger on the Weatherby rifle, which sounded as if a cannon had gone off on the other side of the compound.

Bolan heard the screech of tires as the roar died down. Through the binoculars he saw the guards above the wall turn away. As he waited for the next round, he could practically see Walters working the bolt of the big elephant gun.

The pickup appeared down the street from the compound. Bolan opened the door of the Lincoln and stepped out, slinging the Winchester over his shoulder. He started his sprint across the park as the Ford slowed in front of the wall. In the bed of the pickup, he could see Duke gripping the rim of the small jogging trampoline that had been in his home gym an hour earlier. As the Ford screeched to a halt, the plantation owner jumped from the pickup to the sidewalk in front of the compound.

The Executioner slowed slightly as he stepped off the grass into the street. He watched Duke lay down the trampoline, then dive to the side. Picking up his pace again, Bolan frowned as he neared the sidewalk, timing his last few steps so he could push off with his right foot.

A third massive .416 bullet rang out as the Executioner leapt into the air. Both boots came down on the canvas, and the springs groaned as his weight pushed them downward. He heard a thud as Duke got back into the pickup, then suddenly he was flying into the air toward the top of the wall.

The Ford's tires squealed again as Bolan reached up to catch the wall. Hooking his elbows over the top, he scrambled up and over the barrier, dropped to the walking ledge on the other side and tore the Winchester from his back. Turning to face the courtyard, he saw the house in the center of the compound. A glance at the guard tower to his right told him that the sentry was still focused on the shooting coming from the other side of the fortress.

Bolan turned to eyeball the man in the tower to his left, and as he did, the guard looked his way.

The warrior dived from the wall as the guard brought his FN FAL assault rifle into target acquisition. A short burst of fire sailed over the Executioner's head as he fell from the wall, landing on the grass of the courtyard. He jerked up the Winchester, thumb-cocking the hammer.

A quick shot at the tower forced the guard's head below the concrete barrier.

Sprinting forward again, Bolan worked the lever to chamber another round. The shots had drawn the attention of the man in the other tower, and another burst of rifle fire tore up the grass just to the Executioner's left.

Twisting as he ran, Bolan raised the Winchester one-handed and triggered another bullet at the tower behind him. Again the round struck the concrete just below the gun port, and the guard dropped down out of sight.

Ten yards from the front door of the house, the Executioner dived forward beneath a steady stream of automatic fire. Stroking the lever as he flew through the air, he chambered another round a half second before landing on his belly and sliding across the concrete patio into the door.

As he'd suspected, the firing suddenly stopped as the guards paused to consider the fact that their rounds would now strike the house. As they contemplated their dilemma, the Executioner leaped to his feet, stepped back and kicked the door.

A burly black man wearing a shoulder holster over his gray dress shirt met the Executioner in the doorway, a compact Glock automatic in his fist. As the weapon rose, Bolan brought the stock of his rifle around in an arc, buttstroking the man across the jaw.

A crack echoed against the walls of the entryway as the man dropped to his knees like a felled oak. Bolan brought his own knee up into the man's nose and moved over him as the guard flipped to his back.

Straight ahead, the Executioner saw a winding spiral staircase that led to the second story. Three feet to his right a pair of house guards suddenly appeared in an archway that led to the living room. The first, a wide-shouldered man in a blue sport coat, held a nickel-plated revolver.

Bolan twisted at the waist and shoved the barrel of his rifle against the shiny frame of the revolver. He pulled the trigger, the lever action exploded and the revolver spun away from the guard's hand as he screamed in pain.

The second man opened his mouth in surprise. Bolan took advantage of the delay, bringing the Winchester's barrel around to strike the guard in the side of the head. The force of the blow knocked the man to one side.

The Executioner stepped in. Using the barrel like a lance, he rammed it into the guard's sternum. Air rushed from between the house man's lips as he fell to the floor.

Turning back to the man in the blue sport coat, Bolan reached out, grabbing the back of his head and jamming the Winchester under his chin.

The guard looked down at the weapon, his eyes crossing as he rubbed his injured gun hand.

"Where's Karsimbi?" the Executioner demanded.

The man moved his lips soundlessly.

Passing the Winchester to his left hand, Bolan pulled two rounds from the pocket of his jacket, pressed them against the spring cover and through the loading port. "One more time," he growled. "Where's Karsimbi?"

The Executioner heard movement behind him. Keeping the Winchester under the man's quivering chin, he drew the Browning Hi-Power from his hip, took a half step back and turned.

Another house guard toting a sawed-off shotgun was raising the twin barrels.

A 3-round burst of 9 mm rounds drilled through the guard's chest. He stumbled backward, dancing out of sight into another room.

Turning back to the burly man, Bolan stuck the pistol into his belly. With both guns ready to spit death, the man whispered, "I will take you to him."

"Yes," the Executioner said, "you will."

7

At first Denise LeFevre had been flattered by Hubert Spaak's quest to bed her. Then, as that quest became an obsession, the younger man's attentions grew mildly irritating.

Now, as the actress plodded through the dark jungle night, she was beginning to feel totally repulsed by Spaak. Added to that feeling was a hefty dose of fear. LeFevre had seen a new look in Spaak's eyes that afternoon, which reminded her that she was the only woman with the three men, they were miles from civilization and she was therefore, to a certain extent, at their mercy.

Ahead of her through the dense foliage, LeFevre saw the shadowy outline of Dusty Morrison's cowboy hat. Behind her she could hear the footsteps of Spaak and Streak. Spaak's voice was audible; he was complaining under his breath again. She listened, realizing that under the stress of running for her life, and the proximity she and the others had been forced into, she had begun to truly, completely, and with all her heart, hate the egotistical bastard's guts.

Morrison stepped out of the trees into a small clearing and stopped. LeFevre trudged after him, willing one leg to follow the other, and silently praying that he was getting ready to stop for the night.

As she stepped out from the trees, Morrison turned to her and smiled faintly. "Here," he whispered. "We'll camp here."

The woman took two more steps, then collapsed to a sitting position on the ground.

Spaak and Streak stumbled in. Both of the younger men were as exhausted as she was, she suspected, but only Streak let it show. Denise watched the makeup man fall to his back panting as Spaak came to a halt next to Morrison. Her eyes moved back to the older actor. He had led the way, even checked their position from the tops of several hills while the others rested, all the while exhibiting an energy reserve that defied his age.

LeFevre shook her head as she studied the two men side by side. Both Morrison and Spaak were as macho as they came, but in completely different ways. Spaak's masculinity was forced and overplayed. Dusty, on the other hand was . . . well, Dusty was just *Dusty*. What you saw was what you got, and as he stood tall and erect under the moon in his hat, boots and gun belt, the costume he wore no longer looked like a costume. It was part of the whole package that made up the man—symbolic of the rugged individualism he exhibited whenever they needed him.

Slowly, almost ritualistically, LeFevre pulled her shoes off. They had been walking for hours, and her feet reminded her of that fact. The trek had been made even more unbearable by Spaak's constant complaining and second-guessing of their leader's decisions on which paths to take. She was worn out emotionally, as well as physically, and presumed the others felt the same.

The actress rubbed her feet as she watched Spaak begin to circle the clearing, picking up small pieces of wood.

Morrison turned toward him. "What are you doing?" he asked quietly.

"Gathering firewood," Spaak said.

The older actor shook his head. "No fires tonight."

"Oh, really?" Spaak said, spinning toward him. "It's *night,* Tex, in case you hadn't noticed. You afraid the Apaches will smell the smoke, or what?"

Morrison's voice was patient and controlled, but tinged with a trace of sarcasm. "No, kid," he said. "But I'm afraid the flames will get spotted."

Spaak still held the small pile of sticks he'd gathered. "You learn that in one of those clichéd old Westerns with the fifty-dollar budgets?"

"No, it's basic common sense."

"We'll *freeze* without a fire," Spaak barked.

Morrison shook his head. "We won't freeze. We've got the blankets we brought and it doesn't get that cold out here, anyway."

Spaak looked first at Streak, then LeFevre for support. When he saw he would get it from neither, he slammed the firewood to the ground, then sat down and scowled.

Morrison was suddenly standing in front of Le-Fevre and the woman looked up. The older man smiled, and she saw the sadness in his pale blue eyes. He handed her two blankets, said, "Better get some shut-eye," then moved away.

LeFevre was about to lie down when the sudden roar of an explosion sounded from the direction they'd come from.

"What in the world was that?" Streak almost shouted.

Morrison looked in the direction of the explosion. "Bomb of some kind," he said.

"Nothing gets past you, does it, Sherlock?" Spaak asked.

The actress lay on her back and pulled the blankets over her. As her back touched the ground, dry grass bit into her flesh through her T-shirt, and she rolled to her side. Now the grass jabbed her ribs, and when she laid her head down, it stuck to her face and hair.

Sitting back up, the woman pulled the top blanket off, rolled it into a pillow and lay back down. She closed her eyes as the grass cut into her side again. Well, she was going to hurt and itch no matter what she did, so she might as well get used to it.

That settled, the actress realized the waistband of her tight blue jeans was now cutting into her. It wasn't only uncomfortable, it was exasperating, reminding her of the three pounds she'd gained just before leaving Belgium. Even as tired as she was, she knew if she was going to get any sleep she'd have to at least take off her jeans.

Opening her eyes, LeFevre looked over at Spaak. He lay on his side, facing away from her. Morrison had dropped to his back on the other side of the clearing. With the blanket covering him to the waist and his hat over his face, he looked like something out of one of his movies.

Streak was between the two men. He was still awake, sitting huddled under his blanket and sniffling softly.

Rolling to her back, LeFevre unzipped her jeans, then wiggled them down her hips. Tossing them to the grass next to her, she lay back, closed her eyes and felt sleep engulf her.

AT FIRST the actress thought it was a nightmare. She felt a rough hand mauling her breasts as another hand pulled the crotch of her panties to one side. She heard a rip as the thin fabric split, then the mixed odor of foul breath and sweat filled her sinuses. Lewd, violent gasps echoed in her ear. Something hard stabbed the inside of her thigh, and suddenly she realized she wasn't dreaming.

LeFevre opened her eyes, and Hubert Spaak's lust-filled face looked back at her. He grunted, and his penis rammed against her leg again. The woman opened her mouth to scream, but Spaak's hand moved from her breast to cover her lips. Leaning forward, he pinned her to the ground with his shoulders as she felt his other hand move between her legs to guide himself into her.

She twisted violently to one side, and Spaak rammed into her hip. He cursed under his breath, forcing his knee between hers and rolling her back again. Suddenly the stillness of the jungle night was split by a loud crack.

For a moment Spaak just stared down at her. Then his eyelids dropped, and he rolled off her.

LeFevre looked up to see Dusty Morrison standing over her. The cowboy held the barrel of one of his pistols in his hand. He dropped to one knee, grabbed a blanket and covered her to the waist. "Are you all right?" he whispered gently.

The woman nodded. She looked at Spaak, unconscious at her side. "Is he...dead?"

Morrison leaned over her, pressed a finger into Spaak's neck and shook his head. He turned back to her, and suddenly the woman was in his arms, sobbing.

The cowboy actor held her until the sobs died down, then pushed her tenderly to arm's length. "Better stick close to me, at least the rest of the night," he whispered in his strong, gruff voice. "And I reckon it'd be better if you get your britches on." He stood and turned his back.

When LeFevre was dressed, Morrison turned around, snatched her blankets from the ground and led her back to the spot where he'd been sleeping. He lay one blanket on the ground and rolled the other back into a pillow.

LeFevre lay down and Morrison pulled his own blanket over her to her chin, tucking her in much as her father had done when she was a little girl.

That was the moment Denise LeFevre realized she was in love. And as the gray-haired cowboy leaned over and kissed her on the forehead before lying down with his hat over his face again, she thought she saw a trace of tenderness in his eyes, too.

THE EXECUTIONER holstered the Browning Hi-Power, grabbed the tall house guard by the shoulder and spun him. With the Winchester 94 in his right hand, he ran his left up and down the man's legs, across his chest and around his waist. Finding no more weapons, he jabbed the rifle barrel into the small of his prisoner's back. "Let's go," he ordered.

The guard didn't hesitate. He marched stiffly to the spiral staircase Bolan had seen when he'd entered the house.

The warrior kept one eye on the man's back, the other tilted up the stairs as they wound up the steps. When they reached the second floor the guard led him down a hallway past several closed doors. Reaching the end of the hall, the man stopped.

"Mr. Karsimbi will have me killed if I take you to him," he pleaded without turning.

"And I'll kill you if you don't," the Executioner replied. "So take your choice—now, or later."

The guard reached forward and opened the door.

Bolan shoved the man into the room. He heard a scream, then a small-caliber pistol shot rang out.

The guard fell to the floor.

Without aiming, Bolan fired a round, then worked the lever as he dived forward onto the carpet, the rifle aimed upward. What he saw was almost amusing.

Cringing behind a stuffed reclining chair to one side of a large oak desk was a man not much bigger than Ukewere. He gripped a .22-caliber Colt Woodsman target pistol in both hands.

When he saw the Executioner and the Winchester, the Woodsman tumbled from his shaking hands. "Please. Please don't kill me."

As Bolan rose to his feet, he kept the rifle trained on Karsimbi. "You don't want to die?"

"No...*please*..."

The warrior nodded. "Fair enough. Then we'll agree on a verbal contract. You take me to Big Billy Rukanwe, and you'll live."

The mobster shook his head. "Big Billy? I don't know where Big Billy is."

The Executioner raised the rifle slightly and sighted it on the man's chest. "Then the contract is null and void."

"All right!" Karsimbi shouted. "I'll tell you! I'll tell you!"

The Executioner waved the rifle toward the door. "No," he said. "You'll take me."

The gangster came out from behind the chair. While not a member of the Pygmy race by any standards, he would be pushing it to hit five feet. He wore a canary yellow necktie and a well-cut navy blue suit. His soft kid-leather loafers shuffled across the carpet, his gaze glued to the Executioner.

Bolan poked the rifle into Karsimbi's back. They retraced their steps down the spiral staircase and stepped through the broken front door onto the porch. The warrior reached out with his free hand, grabbing Karsimbi by the back of the neck. "We're going to have to pass your guards in a minute," he said. "I suggest you tell them to set their guns down."

Karsimbi nodded his agreement.

The Executioner prodded him off the porch onto the grass, and they started forward. Fifteen yards from the front gate, Bolan spoke again into the microphone in front of his face. "We're coming out, guys," he said. "It'd be nice if a cab was waiting."

"That's affirmative," Tater Walters replied. "Checker Taxi Service is en route."

Bolan saw the rifles of the tower guards trained on them as they moved on. He grabbed Karsimbi by the collar and stopped the man again. "This would be a great time for a speech," he growled into his ear.

Karsimbi took a deep breath. "Hold your fire!" he shouted. "Don't shoot!"

"Tell them to lay their rifles down," Bolan ordered.

Karsimbi complied, and a second later the men on the wall were unarmed.

Duke's Lincoln pulled up outside the front wall as they reached the gate. Leaning around the man in front of him, the warrior threw the bolt back and swung the gate outward.

Karsimbi moved through the opening, the Executioner at his heels. As they came out from under the wall, Bolan moved closer to the man and cast a quick glance to both towers to make sure the rifles hadn't been picked up again. So far, so good.

Moving around to Karsimbi's front, Bolan spun the man and wrapped an arm around his neck. He dragged the Rwandan gangster backward, the man's heels scraping across the pavement all the way to the rear door of the Lincoln.

Walters was behind the wheel, and he twisted to open the back door. Bolan pushed Karsimbi into the backseat and climbed in after him. The merc floored the accelerator, and the vehicle took off in a cloud of dirt and dust.

The Executioner saw Duke's pickup at the corner a block away, and the Ford fell in behind them as they sped out of the area.

"Where to?" Walters asked.

Bolan hesitated. Duke and Bradfordson had done a good job of delivering the trampoline, but they had exceeded their usefulness. And each step of the way that they tagged along, the two unskilled warriors took a chance of getting killed. He wanted Ukewere with him throughout the remainder of the mission in case he needed the man's contacts. But there was no use risking the lives of the Englishmen.

"Back to Duke's," Bolan replied. "We need to pick up Ukewere, and we'll leave Bradfordson and Duke there."

Walters nodded. "Good idea. But I've got to warn you. Those two are getting their rocks off on the action. They don't understand the inherent dangers, and they won't be easy to dump."

Ten minutes later they were pulling back into the circular drive and parking in front of the house. Bolan sent Walters to fetch Ukewere, told Karsimbi not to move, then got out of the Lincoln and hurried over to the pickup as it slowed.

The Executioner leaned into the open driver's window and spoke to Duke. "We're leaving again as soon as Ukewere gets out here," he said.

"All ready on the western front!" Bradfordson said.

"Tallyho!" Duke added.

Bolan frowned. The two Britons appeared to be having the time of their lives, and it hadn't sunk in yet that they could get killed. But the Executioner knew the hard realities of what could happen on this next leg of the mission, and he didn't want their deaths on his conscience.

"I need you two to stay here," he said. Before they could protest, he added, "We've sent word on to the Belgians that this plantation is a safe haven. They'll be trying to get here on their own. If we miss them, they'll need protection until we can get back. That's where you come in."

Bradfordson nodded, but Duke frowned and said, "How in the name of Queen Lizzie were you able to communicate with them, old chap?"

"No time to explain," Bolan said. "But get inside, grab your favorite guns and batten down the hatches. If you don't hear from us again, it'll mean we found them and got safely out of the country." He turned and walked away before they could say more.

Walters came out of the house trailing Ukewere, the two men heading for the Lincoln. Bolan watched the Twa as they approached the vehicle from opposite sides.

The Executioner frowned. Something was missing, and for a moment he wondered what. Then he realized that the antagonistic expression Ukewere wore like a uniform had vanished. The man looked almost pleasant, and Bolan couldn't help wondering why.

Walters opened the front door and pointed for Ukewere to get in, then took the backseat next to Karsimbi as Bolan slid behind the wheel. The Executioner threw the car in gear. A few moments later he slowed as they neared the road again.

"Okay, Karsimbi," Bolan said. "Which way?"

"I don't know."

Bolan looked into the rearview mirror and stomped the brake. Walters braced his arms on the backseat as Karsimbi flew forward. The Executioner drew the Smith & Wesson, turned and shoved the barrel under the gangster's nose. "Karsimbi, I don't intend to play that game with you now any more than I did back at your house." He cocked the hammer with his thumb. "You're roughly three pounds of trigger pressure away from death, and I suggest you start talking."

A lump appeared in Karsimbi's throat. When he spoke again his voice had risen at least two octaves. "I meant . . . Big Billy has more than one place he hides out when the fighting starts. I know only of one."

Next to the frightened little man, Walters drew his .45 pistols. He placed the barrel of one against Karsimbi's temple; the other he jammed into the man's ribs. "On the count of three?" he asked, looking up at the Executioner.

"One," Bolan said.

Tears began to run down Karsimbi's face. "*Please.* I know only the one, I—"

"Two," the Executioner said.

"You've got to believe me! He has more than one hideout, but I'll take you to the one I know about!"

Bolan lowered the hammer on the revolver but kept it under his prisoner's nose. "Like I asked before, which way?"

"Right," Karsimbi replied shakily. "Turn right."

TWELVE MILES FARTHER EAST along the road to Butare, the Executioner spotted the Isuzu Trooper in the rearview mirror. Walters caught his frown and turned.

"Tutsi troops?" the aging mercenary asked.

"Maybe," Bolan said. "Maybe not." He almost hoped it was Tutsis in the Trooper rather than who he suspected it might be as he drove on.

Spotting a sharp curve ahead, the Executioner waited until he'd rounded it, then stomped the gas. The Lincoln shot forward toward a cluster of large boulders to the right side of the road. Tire tracks led from the road around the back of the rocks, and on the other side of the trail, Bolan saw a paint-chipped green picnic table under a crumbling awning.

With a quick glance in the mirror to make sure the Trooper hadn't yet rounded the curve, the Executioner twisted the wheel and turned off the road. He brought the Lincoln to a halt between the picnic table and the boulders, then turned in the seat to make sure he was out of sight from the road.

"Tater," Bolan said as he got out of the Lincoln, "stay here and watch our friends."

Staying close to the rocks, Bolan hurried to the front of the cluster, then dropped prone with his head facing the road. He heard the Trooper coming before he saw it, then the vehicle flashed around the boulders and continued on toward Butare.

The Executioner felt his blood grow hot. Art Bradfordson sat behind the wheel, and in the passenger's seat he could see Godfrey Duke. The men were singing loudly, and as they passed the boulders Duke raised a quart bottle of whiskey to his lips, then passed it to his partner.

Bolan was on his feet and headed back to the Lincoln a moment later. Ripping open the door, he slid back behind the wheel and threw the transmission into gear.

"Tutsis?" Walters asked as they pulled out from behind the rocks.

The Executioner shook his head as he pulled around the boulders. "No, idiots," he said. "Duke and Bradfordson. Drunk."

Walters knew the problems the Trooper could bring. "If the government troops spot them—"

"They'll be dead," Bolan finished for him. He floored the accelerator as the Lincoln's front wheels hit the road, bringing the vehicle up to a fast eighty miles per hour. The tires squealed as the Executioner guided the car around the curves in pursuit.

Bolan estimated that the Trooper would be a good mile ahead by now. But if he could overtake the two well-meaning but imprudent Englishmen before the Tutsis spotted their Trooper, he might be able to save them.

The Executioner's hopes for a fast rescue vanished as a sudden flurry of gunshots exploded ahead. The sound of screeching tires and screaming metal met his ears as he piloted the Lincoln around another curve, then into a straightaway.

Ahead, perhaps three-quarters of a mile, Bolan saw the Trooper lying on its side just off the roadway. Two more Troopers had pulled up on both sides of the overturned vehicle, and Tutsi soldiers in camouflage fatigues were still shooting into the wreck.

The Executioner leaned hard on the gas pedal, driving the speedometer close to the hundred mark as he raced down the road. Behind him, he heard Walters work the bolt of the Weatherby.

"As soon as we're in range," Bolan said, "take out the closest man."

"Got you," Walters said.

"Ukewere, you and Karsimbi get your heads down." Bolan glanced up into the mirror, then to his side. His words had been wasted. Karsimbi was out of sight in the backseat and Ukewere was already huddled in a fetal position on the floorboard.

A second later the .416 Magnum Weatherby boomed with a deafening roar. Bolan saw a Tutsi facing away from the Lincoln jackknife as he fell to the ground. The heads of the other soldiers snapped toward the oncoming Lincoln.

"Pass me the Winchester, then take out someone else," Bolan ordered. He held his hand up and felt the stock of the Winchester slap into it.

Bolan pulled the rifle over the seat and jammed the stock between his knees. Keeping one hand on the wheel, he used his other to work the lever, then lowered the hammer. Behind him, the big elephant gun roared again and another man dropped.

"Hold on," the Executioner said, then shifted his foot from the accelerator to the brake.

The Lincoln's tires screamed in protest as the brake pads set in. The car slewed sideways, sliding down the asphalt toward the Troopers, then fishtailing back. Bolan fought to keep the vehicle under control as a half dozen FN FAL rifles were aimed at them.

The Lincoln fishtailed the other way, bringing the driver's side around to face the massacre on the road. Bolan drew the big .44 Magnum revolver and got off two thunderous rounds before the vehicle straightened again. Two more of the soldiers fell to the asphalt.

Suddenly the Lincoln stopped. The front and back ends were still trying to settle on the shocks as Bolan holstered the revolver and grabbed the Winchester. He dived from the vehicle as a burst of rounds buzzed over his head, hitting the ground on his shoulder as another volley of fire burrowed holes in the asphalt.

Coming to a halt on his belly, Bolan thumbed the hammer back and triggered a softpoint round that split a soldier's breast bone. The man screamed in pain, then fell next to the front tire of the overturned Trooper.

On the other side of the Lincoln, Walters had abandoned the bolt-action Weatherby for his faster shooting Colts. The Executioner heard an almost steady string of .45 rounds burst from the twin Government Model pistols.

Bolan shifted the Winchester's sights to two men twenty yards ahead of the wreckage. As he aimed at the Tutsi on the right, he saw the hand grenade hanging from the man's battle suspenders. Adjusting his aim, his finger squeezed the trigger.

The softpoint round hit the grenade, and a microsecond later both the man wearing the battle harness and the soldier next to him disintegrated. Bolan ducked his head as shrapnel and bits of flesh rained from the sky. As the rubble from the explosion settled, he looked up again.

The ground was littered with dead soldiers and pieces of the last two men. Silence had fallen over the battlefield, the hum of the idling Lincoln the only sound.

The Executioner rose to his feet, walked to the nearest body and dropped the Winchester next to it.

He pried the FN FAL rifle from the dead fingers, then lifted a half dozen extra magazines from the man's rucksack.

From the corner of his eye Bolan could see Walters had followed his lead, appropriating another of the rifles. "Gather up all the extra ammo, and throw a couple of spare rifles in the trunk," the Executioner said.

He moved toward the chassis of the overturned Trooper, then circled around to the other side. The side of the vehicle had been smashed down with the wreck, and he had to drop to his belly to look into what was left of the window opening.

The Executioner wasn't surprised at what he saw, just saddened.

Bullets had torn Bradfordson's scalp from his head. Other rounds had turned his chest and back into a pin cushion that still oozed blood.

Godfrey Duke had died easier. All but one of the rounds seemed to have missed him. But that one deadly missile of lead had found his heart, and he stared open-eyed back at Bolan, every bit as dead as his fellow Englishman.

"TURN HERE," Karsimbi's shaking voice said from behind Bolan.

The Executioner slowed, turning off the asphalt onto a dirt trail that led into the hills. Karsimbi guided him through several forks in the road and down into a valley. They came to an abrupt dead end surrounded by rocky cliffs and thick foliage.

Bolan threw the transmission into Park and turned around. "I hope for your sake this wasn't a joke."

Karsimbi shook his head. "No, it isn't. But from here, you have to walk."

"Wrong," Bolan answered. "From here, *we* have to walk. How far?"

"One mile," Karsimbi replied. "Maybe a mile and a half." He indicated a steep cliff with his eyes.

All four doors of the Lincoln opened and the men got out. Bolan and Walters pulled out their assault rifles and began to fill their belts and pockets with spare magazines. As they prepared themselves for the hike, the Executioner heard the sound of feet approaching from behind. He turned to see Sal Ukewere.

The man had raised hell about going to see Karsimbi. It had worked out that he wasn't needed, and Bolan had been a little surprised that Ukewere hadn't tried to get away from the plantation while he and Walters were gone. He had been even more surprised that the man hadn't complained about going on to find Big Billy.

As the man looked up at the Executioner, Bolan saw again that the chronic hatred of all he saw seemed to have left Ukewere's face. Had something happened back at the plantation during his absence?

"Can I have a gun?" Ukewere asked.

Bolan looked at the man. "Why?" he asked.

"Because if we're going to get shot at, I want to shoot back," Ukewere said simply.

"Back in Cyangugu, you told me if you had a gun you'd kill me," he reminded the man.

Ukewere's gaze fell to the ground. "I would have," he said. "But that was then. This is now."

Bolan studied the man. Had he really had a change of heart? The Executioner reminded himself that Salewe Ukewere had survived the war-torn nation of Rwanda by being an exceptionally fine con man, and playing both sides of the fence that ran between the Tutsis and Hutus.

Okay, Ukewere might have changed. On the other hand, this could be just another of his well-thought-out hustles.

Ukewere looked back up. "Please," he said. "I want a gun to protect myself." He paused, looked down again, then mumbled something else under his breath.

Bolan frowned. "I didn't here that last part."

"I said, 'And to help you.'"

The warrior reached into his jacket and pulled out the FEG .380 he'd taken from the Tutsi earlier in the day. "Just in case this is a con job, Sal," he said, "you need to be aware of the reality of the situation. You *might* be able to sneak up on me and put a bullet in my back before I kill you. I doubt it, but anything's possible in this world. But if you do, Tater will kill you." He looked over to where the white-haired man was slamming a fresh 20-round magazine into his assault rifle.

Walters had been listening. He raised his weapon and gave Ukewere a smile that would have curdled milk.

Bolan handed the man the .380 butt first.

Karsimbi hurried up next to Ukewere. "I'll need a gun, too," he said.

The Executioner just shook his head, then pointed at the hill with his rifle barrel. "Lead the way," he ordered.

For thirty minutes they climbed the trail leading up out of the valley where they'd left the Lincoln. By now the Executioner was no longer surprised that Walters could scramble up the steep incline over the rocks with the agility of a mountain goat. And Ukewere again showed the same stamina he'd exhibited during their earlier run into Cyangugu. But by the time they reached the summit of the hill, Karsimbi's chest heaved with every breath, and his lips had grown pale.

As he tried to catch his wind, Karsimbi pointed into another valley on the other side of the hill. Bolan followed the man's finger. At the bottom of the slope, partially grown over with weeds, vines and other vegetation, he saw the entrance to an abandoned mine shaft.

Walters stopped between Bolan and Karsimbi. "Gold mine?" he asked.

Karsimbi nodded. When he'd caught enough breath to speak, he said, "Played out years ago."

"And Big Billy's inside?" Bolan asked.

Karsimbi shrugged. "Like I told you, maybe."

The Executioner led the way now, moving as quickly as he could down the steep slope into the valley. The others followed, turning sideways and using the length of their feet to get more traction in the loose earth. When they reached the bottom, Bolan turned to Karsimbi and Ukewere. "You two stay here. And don't waste your time trying to get away. We'll just find you. And if we have to do that, I'll kill you."

Without waiting for an answer, the Executioner moved quickly to one side of the mine opening. Tater Walters took the other side of the hole, his FAL pointed into the air. He looked at Bolan.

The Executioner nodded, and they both darted around the corner into the mine at the same time.

In the semidarkness Bolan could see the remains of rail tracks leading deeper into the mine. He pulled a miniflashlight from his pocket, twisted the beam and moved forward. Twenty yards into the old mine, he could see light coming from a bend in the narrow passage. Staying on the rusted iron rails of the track, he walked silently forward, trailed by Walters.

At the bend in the tunnel, Bolan stopped, then peered around the corner. What he saw made him shake his head in wonder.

The tunnel led into a large cavernous room that had been converted to crude living quarters. At the angle at which he stood, the Executioner could see only part of it, but visible was a king-size bed, a nightstand and a plywood wardrobe. Turning the corner, Bolan walked cautiously down the tunnel, Walters at his heels. When he reached the entrance to the large underground room, he raised the assault rifle to his shoulder and stopped.

From this new vantage point he could see the entire cavern. The area to the left of the bed had been turned into a combination kitchen-dining room. An old kitchen table stood in the center of the space, with four unmatched chairs circling it. Behind it was another table that held a microwave oven attached to a small electric generator. Lining the cave walls were boxes that bore the markings of canned food.

To his right Bolan saw several well-worn couches and chairs that had been set up to form a make-do living room. But it was not what he saw that piqued the Executioner's interest. It was what he heard. To the right of the bed, another tunnel led out of the room, and from it came the running-water sound of a shower.

Bolan crossed the room slowly, careful to peer into every nook and cranny provided by the furniture as he passed. He glanced over his shoulder to see that Walters, ever the good soldier, had taken up a position where he could cover both the room and the tunnel they'd come from. As he reached the passage on the other side, the warrior stopped.

Just around the corner he could hear more than just the water. A deep bass voice was softly singing the signature show tune from the musical *Annie*.

The Executioner stepped around the corner, the barrel of the rifle leading the way. Again, what he saw caused him to shake his head.

A giant black backside faced him. The fat man to whom it belonged stood beneath the faucet of a fifty-five-gallon drum that showered water over the shampoo in his hair.

"Hey, Big Billy," Bolan said.

The man screamed as he jumped straight up in the air. When he came back down, he turned toward the Executioner, madly trying to wash his eyes clear enough to see.

Bolan dropped the barrel of the rifle toward the floor. "Relax. I'm not going to kill you." He paused, then added, "Unless, of course, you don't tell me what I want to know."

8

The Executioner stepped around the corner into the main room as a still-uncertain Big Billy Rukanwe began to dry himself with a towel. "Walters," he called across the room, "I've found him. Go back outside and bring in the other men."

The white-haired merc turned on his heel and disappeared into the tunnel.

Bolan waited until Big Billy had squeezed his corpulent frame into a pair of khaki work pants and a white T-shirt, then followed the man to the living room area of the cavern. As they reached the couches, Walters stuck his head back inside the room. "You'll never believe what Sal found outside," he said.

A moment later, Ukewere shoved Karsimbi through the tunnel opening, then stepped to one side.

A tall, slender woman bearing the traditional tribal markings of the Tutsi entered, holding the hand of a little girl. Bolan glanced at Rukanwe. Big Billy was Hutu, which meant he had a mixed marriage. No wonder he had hiding places all over the country—every time war broke out the radical elements of both tribes would go after his family just as they did Belgians.

Bolan looked at the woman and girl as they walked toward the living area. The little girl was dressed identically to her mother. In one arm she cradled a baby doll.

Rukanwe nodded as he lowered his bulk into a chair. Bolan waited until the woman and little girl had taken seats on one of the couches, then dropped into a chair across from the producer. Walters, Ukewere and Karsimbi joined them, finding seats in the circular pattern of chairs and couches.

Rukanwe's eyes bored holes through Karsimbi. "Judas," he muttered.

"I don't like him much either," Bolan said. "But he didn't have a choice."

Rukanwe turned his attention to his wife and daughter, watching them with nervous eyes.

"I have no intentions of hurting them," the Executioner stated. "Or you, if you tell me what I need to know."

The man's face relaxed, but only slightly.

Bolan came right to the point. "My name is Collier, and I'm looking for the Belgian acting troupe."

The producer looked at the floor. "So are both the Tutsi government and the Hutu rebels. They are probably dead by now."

"I don't know that," Bolan said. "And I want to keep it from happening."

Rukanwe looked up. "Why?"

Bolan looked the man in the eye. "Dusty Morrison is a friend of a friend. I was sent to get him out. As long as I'm here, I might as well get the others to safety, too."

The man nodded. "Your intentions are honorable. But you have no idea how impossible a rescue from Rwanda can be." The man glanced nervously to his wife, then back to the Executioner.

"Nevertheless, I intend to try," Bolan said. "I need to know where they're hiding. And you're the man who can tell me."

Rukanwe used his arms to pry himself from the chair, stood, then turned and faced the wall of the cave. "How do I know I can trust you?" he asked. "How do I know that you, too, do not want to kill my friends?"

"Which tribe do I look like I belong to, Rukanwe, Tutsi or Hutu?"

"Both the Hutus and Tutsis have hired mercenaries before," he replied. Again, he glanced at his wife.

So far the woman hadn't spoken. But Bolan was beginning to suspect there was something Big Billy was afraid she would hear. The man kept looking at her, and his words were coming out only after careful deliberation.

"Does your wife speak English?" Bolan asked.

"I do," the woman stated.

"Then please try to convince your husband that I'm trying to help," the Executioner said to cover the real reason he'd asked the question.

The tall woman stood and moved next to her husband. She looked at Bolan, then said to her husband, "I trust him."

"Why? Why should we trust him?"

"I do not know," the Tutsi woman said. "But I do."

Rukanwe flopped back into his chair. His wife pulled another chair to his side and sat down, motioning the little girl to join them. Big Billy's daughter jumped up and, clutching the doll to her chest, hurried over to her mother's lap.

The producer sucked in a deep breath. "They are in another of my hiding places," he said.

Bolan nodded. Racial prejudice on both sides of the Tutsi-Hutu feud required the Rukanwes to trust no one but themselves. The Executioner sighed. He had seen the same thing the world over. Every race on the face of the planet had its share of racial prejudice, but nowhere was it any more pronounced than in Rwanda.

"So, where is this hideout?" Bolan asked.

"In the Rugege Forest," Rukanwe said. "But there are only four of the original cast who survived the attack at the theater. He paused for a moment. "Dusty Morrison was one of them. It was his guns that allowed even those four to escape."

"The Rugege is a big place," Bolan said. "Where in the forest are they?"

"I have an underground house there that is equipped for long stays." Again he looked nervously at his wife.

The Executioner frowned as he looked around the cave. "So how come *you* didn't go there?" he asked. "It sounds more isolated and probably more comfortable than this place."

Rukanwe was almost shaking as he watched the woman at his side. When he spoke, it was as if the words had to be pried from his mouth with pliers.

"We . . . went there last time," he said. "I was afraid someone would know of it."

The Executioner studied the man closely. That might be part of it, but there had to be more. Two and two wasn't quite adding up to four yet. Bolan looked at the woman. "Mrs. Rukanwe, could you and the child excuse us for a few moments? I'd like to talk to your husband privately."

The Tutsi woman looked at her husband. Big Billy looked relieved as he nodded. Mrs. Rukanwe patted her husband on the hand, stood and led the little girl out of the cave into the tunnel.

"Tell me the truth now," Bolan said as soon as she was gone. "There's more, and I know it."

Rukanwe's eyes had been an overstressed water dam waiting to burst. Tears suddenly flooded his face and he leaned forward, clasping his hands over his eyes. His entire body shook with sobs when he said, "It is *I* who am the Judas, not Karsimbi. I am a traitor to my friends!"

Bolan waited until the man calmed down, then said, "Tell me what happened."

The producer sat back up and wiped his face with the back of his arms. "As I left the forest after delivering the troupe," he stated. "I was stopped by Tutsi soldiers. One of the men recognized me, and they knew I had to know where the actors were." He paused to wipe his running nose, then went on. "They not only threatened to kill me, Mr. Collier, but also my wife and child! So . . . so . . . So I told them where the house was located!" He broke into tears once more and buried his face into his hands.

The Executioner stood. "I'll need directions to the house," he said, lifting the rifle from where he'd leaned it against his chair.

His face still hidden by his hands, Rukanwe shook his head. "It is too late," he moaned softly. "By now they are dead."

"Maybe not. In any case, we've got to find out. How do we get there?"

Rukanwe's hands dropped to his lap and he looked up, his features a masterpiece of spiritual misery. "I will take you there, Mr. Collier," he said. "It is the least I can do after what I have already done."

DEPRESSION WASN'T PART of Mack Bolan's psychological profile. Even as a young soldier in the jungles of Southeast Asia, he had instinctively recognized despondency as an enemy that stood in the way of a success as substantially as the Vietcong or NVA regulars. He had learned early on to force dejection from his soul whenever it threatened to raise its ugly head.

No matter how long the odds or how hopeless a predicament appeared, Bolan knew that a positive outlook was always more productive.

The Executioner's willpower in this area, however, was tested to the limit as he walked up on the remains of the underground house.

Bolan stood at the edge of the trees, letting his eyes take in the wreckage he saw before him. The evidence that Rukanwe's underground house had once hidden in this clearing was everywhere: in the scraps of lumber, the slivers of steel support rods, the pieces of drywall and the white drywall dust that now mixed with the damp earth.

The producer stepped out of the trees and stood at the Executioner's side. "Oh my God," he said softly.

Bolan moved into the clearing. Charred pages from books, components from electronic devices, torn upholstery and splinters of furniture lay within the giant cavity that now gaped in the jungle floor. The concrete staircase leading down from what had once been the hidden entrance appeared to be the only thing left intact. Slowly the Executioner descended the steps, stepping over more rubble as he went. He reached an area that looked to have been a living room, and amid the wreckage saw the remains of a television set lying on the blistered carpet. Bits of plastic from videotapes covered the remains like black hailstones that wouldn't melt, and more pages from what had to have been a fairly extensive library fluttered in the scant breeze.

Moving on into what had once been a kitchen, Bolan saw exploded cans of beans, vegetables and other foodstuffs, their contents covering the floor and what remained of the walls. The plumbing in the bathroom had been ripped from within the walls, and the water from a hidden tank had gushed out to cover the floor ankle deep.

In the bedroom, the Executioner saw wet bed springs, mattress stuffing and feathers lying in the water that had run down the hall and entered the room. Both men's and women's clothing—some intact, some blown to pieces—lay beneath the already-stagnant puddles.

The Executioner looked up to see Rukanwe standing at the edge of the hole, his chest heaving with sobs as he stared down in horror. "What were they wearing?" Bolan called up.

The producer looked down at him without answering.

"What were they *wearing,* Rukanwe?" Bolan asked again.

He seemed to come out of a trance. "The men still had on their costumes when we got here," he said. "Tuxedos ... But Morrison had on his cowboy suit. Boots, chaps, spurs ... that sort of thing."

Bolan glanced at a black bow tie next to his feet. "Did they have other clothes with them?"

Rukanwe seemed to have sunk into his trance of guilt once more. He said nothing.

"You want to make up for what you did?" the Executioner asked.

The producer nodded.

"Then snap out of it, get a grip on yourself and answer my questions." He paused, then repeated, "Did they have other clothes with them?"

Big Billy nodded.

Bolan began wading through the mess, his eyes searching the floor. He had already seen pieces that might have once been tuxedos, as well as shreds of material that sparkled with sequins and would have been an evening gown. And as his eyes continued to roam, he saw two large silver Mexican spurs. One lay intact in the corner. The other had been blown apart, with the shank, rowel and band gleaming up through the water from various parts of the room.

The futility that the Executioner had fought against upon seeing the destruction began to fade. True, the Tutsi soldiers had destroyed the underground house with the same savagery with which they destroyed the Hutus—and the Hutus destroyed them—but they *hadn't* destroyed Dusty Morrison or the other surviving members of the troupe. At least not yet.

Nowhere in the wreckage of Big Billy's underground hideout did Bolan see a trace of anything human. And regardless of how heavy the explosives used had been, there would be at least some body parts that were still identifiable.

"John!" Walters's voice called from somewhere above. "Tracks!"

Bolan moved to the edge of the bedroom, reached up and hauled himself up to ground level. Walters stood at the opposite edge of the clearing, and he jogged to the white-haired mercenary's side.

The merc pointed down at a heelprint in the soft earth. Small, probably a woman's shoe, it had a zig-zag pattern typically found on athletic footwear. Just beyond it a vine growing along the floor of the forest had been broken almost in two, and next to it the Executioner saw a print that could only have been made by a cowboy boot.

Bolan turned back to the clearing where Rukanwe, Ukewere and Karsimbi stood next to the hole in the ground. "Rukanwe, you and Karsimbi head back. Ukewere, come with me."

Karsimbi looked up at him. "We'll need the keys to the car."

Bolan shook his head. "Walk. You'll make it. And it'll be just that much longer before you can alert the Tutsi troops to the fact that we're here."

"I would never do that," the producer vowed.

"I believe you wouldn't want to," Bolan replied. "But you already did once. So maybe you wouldn't do it again, but your little friend wouldn't hesitate."

Karsimbi looked up at the Executioner, his eyes frightened. "But there are animals in this forest," he stated. "What if we come across a lion?"

"Then you'll be eaten," Bolan said simply.

"But—"

"There's one other alternative." The Executioner drew the big .44 Magnum revolver. "I can kill you where you stand."

Without further argument, Karsimbi and Rukanwe turned and hurried back toward the trees.

Bolan watched them go, taking a second to compare the two men. There was a difference. Karsimbi was an opportunistic little gangster with no morals. He'd inform on them in a heartbeat if he saw any profit in it.

Rukanwe, on the other hand, had been a decent, ordinary man who found himself in extraordinary circumstances. Big Billy had given up his friends to save his family. That didn't make it right, and the blood of Dusty Morrison and the Belgians would still be on Rukanwe's head if the Executioner didn't find them in time. But it did make a difference.

The Executioner turned back to where Walters and Ukewere were waiting at the edge of the trees. If they could find the actors' tracks as easily as they had, then so could the Tutsi soldiers. And the Rwandan government troops had a head start.

With a quick look at his two companions, Bolan said, "Let's go," then led the way deeper into the forest.

THE TRANSFORMATION hadn't been sudden, nor was it yet complete. But it *was* going on. Somehow, he was changing, and Salewe Ukewere knew it. He watched the big man ahead of him as they made their way through the thick trees. Yes, he was changing. Or, perhaps he should say, he was *being* changed.

And the catalyst of that change was the big man in front of him.

Ukewere stepped over the thick roots of a tree and moved on. Behind him, he could hear the soft steady breathing of Tater Walters. There had been a time when he had thought of Walters as no different than himself. Walters bought and sold information just as Ukewere did. But the white-haired man had never dealt with the Tutsis or Hutus, peddling his intelligence only to American agencies like the CIA.

Even in a war-ravaged nation like Rwanda, Walters had kept his values. The man had a code of honor that he didn't violate, and that, Ukewere realized as he ducked under a low-hanging limb, was the difference between Walters and himself: a code of honor, a system of doing things that took into consideration the rights of other people. Ukewere had been taught a code like that as a child, but had abandoned it after his parents' murders. Since then he had thought of no one's welfare except his own.

Ahead, Bolan stopped suddenly, raising a hand and cocking an ear. Ukewere and Walters stopped immediately. The African heard the faint rustling of leaves ahead and to their right. He gripped his gun as his heart jumped to his throat.

Then a jungle rat darted across their path to disappear again in the thick foliage. Bolan moved on. Ukewere and Walters followed.

Ukewere watched the jungle floor as they walked. The Belgians and the American cowboy with them knew nothing of covering their trail, and the Tutsi troops who had followed had seen no need to do so, either. The ground was a mass of broken sticks and vines that pointed the way as clearly as road signs.

Ukewere followed his two companions down an embankment and across a narrow trickling stream. The big American stopped, then squatted to look at a print in the mud. Ukewere moved up next to him and saw the prints of several combat boots.

Just to the side of the mass was a slightly different impression, another boot, but this one lacked the lug soles of the Tutsi soldiers' footwear. The toe was more pointed, and the heel had sunk far deeper into the mud than the sole.

The African followed the two men up the other side of the bank and they moved on. Collier was a good tracker, and he wondered where the big white man had learned the skill. He himself had been taught by his father and uncles as a child, sometime during the period when they had also taught him the use of traditional weapons of the tribe, such as the bow, spear and blowgun.

The memory of his early weapons education caused Ukewere to look ahead at the rifle under Collier's right arm. Behind him, Walters carried an identical weapon. His hand moved to the small pistol stuck in his belt, and he let his fingers run along the checkered plastic grip.

Ukewere had never fired a gun, and he was glad that Collier had given him the small one. The rifles looked heavy and complicated. You could shoot the little pistol in his belt by simply pulling the trigger, Collier had said—it was double action, whatever that meant.

The big American paused as they reached another break in the trees. Ukewere saw him study the open area ahead for several seconds, then move cautiously into the clearing. Ukewere followed, his hand still on the grips of the pistol. When they reached cover once again Ukewere let his arm fall back to his side.

How did you point a pistol? Collier had said to line up the sights, and he knew those were the black things on top of the gun, at the front and back. But how exactly did you do it? With a blowgun you just pointed, and he supposed that would work with a firearm as well. In any case, that was the method he would have to employ if he was forced to shoot at someone. He would just have to do it and hope for the best.

The thought of a blowgun took his mind into the past once more, to his father and his father's two brothers. His uncles had tried to talk him into fleeing to Zaire after his parents' murders. For centuries the Twa of Rwanda had joined their cousins in the neighboring country when war broke out at home. In Zaire the Twa had resisted all government attempts to integrate them into mainstream society. The Twa of that country still lived in the mountains and jungles—as the tribe should, according to his father's brothers.

Ukewere had refused the offer to go with his uncles, choosing instead to stay and avenge his parents in the only way he knew how.

Collier bent to study more tracks, and Ukewere saw him lift something white. He looked closer and saw it was the butt end of a cigarette. The big man turned to him and Walters. "We're close," he mouthed silently. "It's still warm." He took off again, moving even more slowly and more precisely now.

Ukewere felt the tension mount in his chest. They would come upon the Tutsi soldiers, and they would come upon them soon. How would he fare? Would he fight valiantly as did the Twa heroes in the stories he had listened to as a child? Or would he panic and flee like the cowards also contained in those stories? He had been trained in weapons, yes, but he had never before faced a man with them. He had avenged the murders of his parents by trickery rather than confrontation, and although he knew he was responsible for the deaths of many Hutu and Tutsi, those deaths had come from information he had sold, not fighting.

He had sold the information, but others had done his killing for him. How would he behave in a face-to-face encounter with an armed adversary?

Suddenly, as they moved on through the Rugege Forest to meet their enemy, Ukewere realized that his transformation had been completed. He might not know yet how he would react to actual battle, but he knew he could no longer engage in the long-distance assassination of faceless men. The men who had died because of him, both Hutu and Tutsi, had more than likely not been the individuals responsible for his parents' deaths. They were just men—like himself—who had been caught up in the carnage that had infected the land since the Tutsis and Hutus had arrived.

These men—both Hutu and Tutsi—murdered, raped and looted, and their acts were shameful. But they were no more shameful than the acts of Salewe Ukewere. The Tutsi slaughtered the Hutu because they were Hutu. The Hutu butchered the Tutsi for being Tutsi. Ukewere had orchestrated the deaths of men and women from both tribes for the same bigoted reasons.

Bolan stopped suddenly and raised his hand again.

Ukewere froze. He listened, but heard nothing. He looked, but saw nothing in the thick foliage on the other side of the big man.

As he strained to see whatever it was that had caused the big man to stop again, Ukewere came to another sudden realization. He knew he could never again go back to the long-range assassination of Hutus and Tutsis he didn't even know. He suspected he would go on fighting injustice, and in that way continue to try to avenge the deaths of his mother and father. But from this day on he must distinguish between the Tutsis and Hutus who were responsible for the bloodshed in his country, and those who were victims.

In short, Ukewere realized, he wanted to become more like this man who called himself Collier.

Suddenly it dawned on the African that what had stopped Collier couldn't be seen or heard, for it had been neither sight nor sound.

The odor had been infiltrating his nostrils since Collier held up his hand, but only now did Ukewere's brain identify it as out of place. Smoke. Cigarette smoke.

His hand trembling, Ukewere drew the pistol from his belt.

DUSTY MORRISON WATCHED the sun peek through the thick trees and saw Streak rise to a sitting position under his blankets. The makeup artist looked sick as he rubbed his eyes. Morrison knew how he felt, and thought of the immortal words of W. C. Fields: "I feel like the Russian army's been walking over my tongue in their stocking feet." He couldn't remember which movie the line had come from, but it had been the great comedian's description of a hangover.

Well, Morrison didn't have a hangover, hadn't even had a beer in maybe twenty years. And his mouth wasn't particularly dry, although he could use a drink of water. But every muscle, bone and joint in his body ached, and his eyelids felt as if they each weighed twenty pounds. So when Streak rose to his feet, walked over and asked how he was feeling, he altered Fields's words slightly. "Like the Russian army's been walking over my body in iron boots."

Streak caught the line, gave a weak, frightened smile and shuffled off into the trees to relieve himself.

Morrison looked across the clearing to where Spaak still lay huddled under his blanket. The would-be rapist was responsible for the older actor's heavy eyelids. Morrison had found sleep impossible after what the arrogant young man had tried to do to Denise, and had lain awake all night watching to make sure Spaak didn't try a repeat performance. His vigilance had been unneeded. Spaak had awakened sometime during the wee hours of the morning, gone into the bushes to do what Morrison assumed Streak was doing now, then returned to his blanket. Otherwise he'd just lain there quietly.

Feeling Denise rustle at his side, Morrison forced himself to his feet as quickly as his aching body would allow. He began to gather up the blankets and other supplies they'd unpacked for the night and tucked them into the backpacks. Out of the corner of his eye he saw Spaak awaken and sit up.

The man rubbed the back of his head and glared at Morrison, who was more than happy that Spaak's head hurt. He deserved more than that for what he tried to pull.

LeFevre stood and began to roll up her blankets, and the confused mixture of emotions Morrison had felt all night intensified. He drew the ten-inch bowie knife from the sheath on his Buscadero rig and knelt on the ground. Digging in the dirt, he busied himself burying the empty cans of food they'd opened. He didn't want to look at the woman—he knew how it would make him feel. He was confused, and a little voice in his head told him that at this point it would be better to stay confused than confront the bewilderment in his soul.

All night, as he lay awake, he had pondered why Denise reminded him so of Lois. They looked nothing alike. They acted nothing alike. Denise had a Belgian accent, and Lois had been from Kansas, with a typical Midwest lack of any accent.

So what was the connection between the two women? Ever since he'd handed Denise his blanket after the attempted rape, and their eyes had met, his brain had fought against facing the answer that his heart already knew. But now, as Dusty Morrison stood up from the ground and felt the ache in both knees, he could escape reality no more.

The reason Denise LeFevre kept making him think of Lois was simple: he had been in love with Lois, and now he was in love with Denise LeFevre.

The immediate guilt that followed the acceptance of his feelings swept over the man like some massive tidal wave. His weary bones ached more. The twenty-pound weights on his eyelids became forties. He could barely force his legs to hold him upright, and when he tried to walk those same limbs refused the command.

Then Streak stepped back out of the trees zipping up his pants, and it dawned on Morrison that even in the midst of the worst guilt he had ever felt in his life, something had reawakened in his soul that had been asleep for a year.

Morrison was no longer apathetic about his life. For the first time since Lois had died, he cared whether he lived or died. And he wanted more than anything else in the world to go on living.

When the other three had finished packing, they turned to Morrison, who said, "Ready?"

Streak and LeFevre nodded. Spaak turned his head to one side but didn't say anything.

Morrison started into the trees. As his boots clomped over both dry and green leafage on the forest floor, he felt his heart begin to lighten from the guilt. It was as if life were about to start anew.

A hand touched his shoulder.

"Are you okay?" Streak asked, his voice trembling in fear. It was only at that moment that Morrison realized he had stopped dead.

The aging actor felt the grin break across his face. "I'm fine," he said, then chuckled. He felt twenty years old again.

LeFevre squeezed his arm. "I love you," she whispered. "Dusty, I love you."

Morrison nodded, wondering now if the joy he felt in his heart might overwhelm him. "I love you, too," he said, taking her into his arms. "So what do you say we get out of here and start a life somewhere?"

LeFevre smiled up into his eyes. Taking her hand, Morrison started forward again through the Rugege Forest. Where he was going, he had no idea. What he would do when he got there, he didn't know. But he did know that his heart was lighter, and he was happier than he'd been since that day so long ago when the doctor had brought him the bad news about Lois.

Which was why it seemed like such incredibly bad timing when the men with the rifles suddenly appeared through the trees.

9

The first tangible sign of the enemy might have been the cigarette smoke, but the Executioner had known he was close a good five minutes before he smelled the smoke.

Innate ability, intense training and experience often combined to produce skills in a warrior far beyond what could be explained.

The Executioner had sensed the sentry's presence for a hundred yards before the smoke drifted his way. What had spawned his awareness? He didn't know. Exactly how he had become aware of the man's presence would forever remain a mystery known only to his subconscious mind.

But he knew the man was there.

Bolan waited, listening, his hand in the air to halt both Ukewere and Walters. A faint rustling sounded through the trees, and he waited for it again. The sound was familiar—the brush of a lightweight BDU blouse sleeve rubbing against more of the same material.

Turning to Ukewere, Bolan handed the man his rifle, then stooped to whisper in the man's ear. "Stay here. I'll be back for you."

Ukewere looked down at the rifle in his hands as if it were a rattlesnake.

Looking up and behind the little man, Bolan saw Walters frozen in place. With hand signs he told the merc to explain the workings of the battle rifle to Ukewere, then turned back toward where the enemy awaited him.

The Executioner drew the heavy Smith & Wesson .44 Magnum revolver and dropped to his hands and knees. Careful to keep the weapon out of the damp dirt, he moved slowly forward through the thick undergrowth of the jungle. Bolan's nostrils flared like those of a bloodhound as he followed the cigarette-smoke trail that linked him to the man marked for death.

Twenty yards farther into the trees, leaves and vines, Bolan saw a flicker. He froze, watching, waiting to see more. It looked as if the leaves themselves were moving—not an uncommon sight in the thin breezes that invaded the thick jungle.

But something was different. Something was out of place.

The Executioner continued to watch patiently until he saw the movement again. His eyes focused on the spot, and he saw that the moving leaves weren't leaves at all. All around the area of movement, the leaves and vines were a bright jungle green. But the area that moved was a darker brown and looked more like a tree limb covered with bark, which was exactly what tree-bark camouflage fatigues were designed to look like.

The Executioner moved forward on all fours. He made his way around several trees, taking a circuitous route toward the man who had chosen the wrong camouflage gear.

By the time he was within ten yards of the movement, the Executioner could see the man sitting with his back against the tree trunk. The tall, slender Tutsi was alone, which meant he'd been posted as a rear sentry while the other soldiers rested.

The orange glow of the cigarette tip moved in an arc from the man's mouth back to his lap where his forearm rested on his thigh. In addition to the tree-bark cammies, Bolan could now see that the man wore a leather garrison belt and flap holster. An FN FAL assault rifle leaned against the tree trunk next to him.

Employing all the stealth he could muster, the warrior crept forward until he was less than three feet from the unsuspecting sentry. In one fluid motion, Bolan rose to his feet, swinging the heavy .44 Magnum revolver in an arc that struck the soldier against the temple. Without a sound he dropped to the forest floor.

Bolan lifted the assault rifle and pulled two more magazines from the holder on the sentry's garrison belt, then hurried back to where Ukewere and Walters waited. The African was sighting down the barrel of the rifle Bolan had given him.

"You feel like you can use it?" the Executioner asked.

Ukewere looked at him, his eyes betraying his doubt.

"How about the pistol?" Bolan asked.

The man nodded, his expression displaying more confidence this time.

The Executioner nodded. "Then leave the rifle. We'll pick up another one in a few minutes." He turned to Walters. "Tater, I took out the sentry. The others must be close. I'm going to circle to the front— they'll have another man posted there. Take Sal and move in from the rear. Give me twenty minutes, then wait until you hear the first shot."

He turned back to the African. "You can stay clear if you want to, Sal."

Ukewere shook his head.

Bolan studied the man's eyes. There *had* been a change. He didn't know exactly when, where or why, but Ukewere was no longer the bitter, antagonistic, self-centered semioutlaw he had been when Bolan had first met him.

"Okay, then," the Executioner said. "Let's move out."

THE HUTU TRIBESMEN who stepped out of the trees were as surprised to see Dusty Morrison and the Belgians as the acting troupe was to see them.

Morrison pushed LeFevre to the ground, drawing the twin Colt .45 Peacemakers.

A short, stocky black man wearing multicolored tribal robes started to raise the assault rifle he held. Morrison thumbed back the hammer of the .45 in his right hand, and a split second later the Peacemaker fired its load.

The man in the colorful robe dropped the rifle. He screamed as tiny dots of blood appeared just below his chin in the V-shaped opening of the robe. The man looked down at his chest, now peppered with red where the bird shot had struck.

Another robed figure stepped forward and aimed a pistol Morrison's way. The aging actor shifted slightly, firing again with the Colt in his left hand. More bird shot flew from the Peacemaker, catching the tribesman in the face from roughly six feet away. This man made no sound.

Morrison saw the blood in the man's right eye and knew at least one of the tiny pellets had entered the optic nerve. Then the man's eyes rolled back in his head and he fell forward onto his face.

Raising both single-action revolvers, Morrison aimed at the remaining two Hutus. He had thumbed both hammers back when he felt the jolt in the back of his neck.

Fire raced through the actor's brain as he fell to his knees. He tried to focus his blurred vision on the ground in front of him, but his eyes refused to steady. Behind him, he heard Spaak scream, "Don't shoot! I stopped him! Don't kill us!"

The rattle of automatic fire threatened to burst the aging cowboy's eardrums. Unseen to his rear, Spaak screamed again. But this time the Belgian actor's scream was one of pain.

Morrison saw a blurry pair of bare feet move into view in front of him. He tried to get up, but the pain in the back of his head stopped him cold. He saw what happened next in slow motion.

One of the feet rose off the ground. The robe parted to reveal a knee and part of a thigh, then the knee struck under the cowboy's chin and sent him flipping onto his back.

Strangely the new blow washed the waves from Morrison's eyes. He could see clearly now as more feet moved in at his sides. He tried to move, but his arms and legs wouldn't cooperate. A sharp tingling raced through his outstretched limbs as if they'd gone to sleep and the blood was just now rushing back into them. He watched the angry face above him flip the rifle over in his hands and raise it high into the air.

Again, Morrison tried to roll out of the way. Again, he couldn't make his body follow the orders from his brain. He watched the rifle butt all the way to his face, then he closed his eyes.

FIFTY YARDS AHEAD of where the sentry in the tree-bark camouflage now lay, Bolan heard the rest of the Tutsi soldiers resting in the forest. Their voices were low, hushed, but now and then a loud laugh broke the stillness. Each time that happened the Executioner heard what he perceived to be an admonishment in Kinyarwanda.

Bolan skirted wide around the men, making his way through the dense foliage as quickly as silence allowed. As he darted from tree to tree he caught brief glimpses of heads, arms, elbows and knees. The men appeared to be seated in a circle, their backs against the tree trunks.

The Executioner moved twenty yards in front of the assemblage, then slowed when he sensed a new presence to his side. Slinging the assault rifle over his back, he dropped to his belly, pulling himself forward with his elbows. When he reached a wide boulder, he jerked several handfuls of long grass from the ground and wove it through his hair.

Bolan rose slightly, peering just over the top of the boulder. Unlike his counterpart to the rear, the point guard was alert. He stood with rifle ready, turning frequently to check all sides. He didn't smoke, either.

Dropping back behind the boulder, the warrior considered the situation. The man stood in the center of a clearing, a good ten yards away. There was no cover after the boulder, and unless the guard moved closer to the trees on another side of the open area, there was no sense in trying to move around him.

Bolan's eyes scanned the forest floor for a rock or limb, anything small enough to throw. Seeing nothing, he pulled one of the spare FAL magazines from his belt and thumbed off the top round. He risked one more quick glance over the boulder and saw that the man had turned again. He still faced away from the Executioner, but now stood at a slight angle.

Rising slightly higher, Bolan drew back his arm and cast the bullet over the man's head, across the clearing and into the trees. The round struck a tree trunk just to the guard's left, causing him to twist that way.

He now faced directly away from the Executioner.

Bolan was over the boulder before the guard knew what had caused the sound in the forest. Swinging the assault rifle, he smashed the stock against the back of the man's head. The guard dropped to the ground as blood spurted from the wound.

The warrior moved quickly now, making his way back through the forest toward where the rest of the

Tutsi soldiers sat. He heard the laughter again, then moved behind a pair of trees that had grown together two feet over his head. Peering between the trunks, he could see the faces of two men who sat with their backs against a trunk.

One of the men had a beard cropped close to his face. His rifle rested across his lap. The other man wore a tree-bark camouflage BDU cap over frizzy black hair that stuck out from the sides. His weapon leaned against the tree to his side.

Projecting from the sides of a tree facing the two men were the arms and knees of another pair of Tutsi soldiers. A fifth man sat cross-legged on the open ground to the left. A sixth reclined on his elbows just beyond him.

Bolan looked past the men and saw a small rustling in the trees. Walters and Ukewere were in place. They'd be together; the aging mercenary was a pro, and he'd have kept an inexperienced fighter like Ukewere close to him.

The Executioner moved away from the intertwined trees, taking up a position at a forty-five-degree angle from where he'd seen the movement. The last thing they needed was to kill one another in a cross fire. Slowly, methodically, he unslung the assault rifle and flipped the selector to semiauto.

Taking careful aim on the bearded man, Bolan drew a deep breath, let half of it out and squeezed the trigger. The bullet struck its target squarely between the eyes and made the top of its head disappear.

The rest of the soldiers froze in stunned surprise. Bolan took advantage of their shock to swing the rifle to one side, sighting in on the man in the BDU cap. His next round took the Tutsi in the center of the chest. Before the body had quit its death throes, the Executioner was moving out into the clearing.

He heard the sound of Walters's rifle on full-auto as he flipped his own weapon to "rock and roll." A quick burst of fire caused the man sitting in the open to jerk in a macabre dance of death. Another volley of rounds took out his reclining companion.

The Executioner moved farther into the open, twisting to fire at the final two men on the other side of the tree trunk. Before he could pull the trigger, he saw both of them fall to Walters's withering blasts of fire.

Sudden silence replaced the booming explosions of the guns.

THE TRAIL LEFT by Dusty Morrison and the Belgians hadn't been hard to pick up again. And had the Tutsi soldiers known how close their prey had been, Bolan doubted they would have chosen to stop and rest.

Morrison and the rest of the company had escaped the Tutsis, but they hadn't escaped the Hutu rebel force that the Executioner now saw as he peered down through the thick leaves and vines.

From his vantage point near the top of a tall tree, the Executioner watched the valley a hundred yards away through his minibinoculars. Four men in bright tribal robes sat in a circle just to the side of the bound and blindfolded actors. They appeared to be in the midst of a heated discussion. Faint traces of blood were visible on the chest of one of the men.

Two other men—one white and wearing blue jeans, the other black and dressed in Hutu robes—lay on the ground to the side of the circle, apparently dead.

Bolan shifted the binoculars slightly and saw Dusty Morrison's trademark ten-gallon hat, pulled low above the blindfold. The actor still wore his boots, chaps and an empty hand-tooled Buscadero-style gun belt sporting sterling-silver studs and buckles.

The Executioner squinted through the glasses. Dried blood caked the cowboy's face around the blindfold.

Next to Morrison, Bolan saw a smaller man with a thin goatee hanging beneath the black cloth tied over his face. The man's frail shoulders were shivering in fear. On his other side sat a woman in blue jeans and a T-shirt. She, too, was blindfolded, and her hands had been tied behind her back.

Bolan passed the binoculars to Tater Walters, who sat on the limb next to him. As the white-haired merc studied the scene below, the Executioner looked down at Ukewere on the ground. "Pass up our rifles," he whispered.

Ukewere did as ordered.

Walters handed the binoculars back to Bolan. "Think they're trying to decide whether to kill them or not?" he asked.

The Executioner shook his head. "That's a foregone conclusion. They're just trying to decide how to do it."

Walters nodded as he took the rifle Bolan extended to him. He looked down at it, then back up to the Executioner. "We need a couple of decent bolt actions and scopes for this, you know."

"The Rugege Forest sporting goods store is closed, Tater," Bolan said as he lifted the stock of his own rifle to his shoulder. "Start on the left and work your way toward the middle. I'll start on the right."

"That's affirmative."

In his peripheral vision Bolan saw the merc jam the stock of the assault rifle into his shoulder and sight down the barrel.

The man on the right sat almost full profile to the Executioner. Bolan's first shot drilled through his temple, blowing blood, brains and bone fragments out the other side of his head to shower over the face of the man seated at his side. The man's hands shot up instinctively to wipe away the gore.

The Executioner dropped the front sight on the back of one of the man's hands. To his side, Walters's weapon exploded. Squeezing the trigger again, Bolan saw the Hutu's little finger fly off just before the bullet went on through the skull.

As he moved the sights toward the third Hutu in the circle, Bolan saw Walters's first target stretched out on the ground. He and his companion pulled their triggers simultaneously, and the Executioner's next round entered the Hutu rebel's throat and severed the jugular vein.

Walters's round exploded through the man's heart. Blood shot from both wounds as if they were open fire hydrants.

Bolan slung the rifle over his shoulder, grasped the branch beneath his hips with both hands and started to swing down out of the tree. He stopped when he saw the flicker of color on the hill just beyond the valley where the actors sat in blind confusion.

Focusing on the color, Bolan saw it was a Hutu robe. The head and shoulders of a man appeared, then his waist, and finally his feet as he sprinted over the crest of the hill.

A second later two dozen more Hutu rebels followed. All carried FN FAL assault rifles.

"Sal, stay here!" Bolan shouted as he launched himself from the limb.

He heard Walters drop to the ground behind him as he landed on his feet. "Let's go, Tater. We've got to get them out of there before the rebels reach the valley."

Dodging tree trunks and hurdling logs, stumps and boulders, the two men sprinted forward through the forest. When they reached the valley, Bolan saw the first of the rebels leading the others down the hill. The man was still a good two hundred yards away, but closing the gap fast. The rest of the Hutus were only a few feet to his rear.

Bolan snapped a hip-shot up the hill as he raced forward toward the blindfolded actors. The shot flew wide, but hit close enough to the leader to slow his pace. Reaching Dusty Morrison, the Executioner ripped the blindfold from the actor's face and jerked the man to his feet. "My hands," Morrison began, "they're tied behind—"

"No time to worry about that now," Bolan said as he reached down and hefted the woman over his left shoulder. "Can you run?"

Morrison nodded.

"Then do it."

Bolan pushed the cowboy ahead of him toward the other side of the valley. He turned and fired a one-handed volley of rounds up the hill as Walters draped the goateed man over his shoulder.

Two of the Hutus fell to the ground. The others stopped in their tracks.

Turning back toward where he'd left Ukewere, Bolan saw Morrison running awkwardly, his bound hands in tight fists behind his back. The Executioner sprinted after the cowboy as the first burst of return fire ripped chunks of grass and earth from the ground around his feet. Just behind him and to his rear, Bolan could hear Walters's labored breathing as he carried the other man.

The Executioner ran on, twisting back to fire again with one hand, his rounds dropping another of the Hutu rebels. Turning back to the trees, he saw Ukewere suddenly step out from cover.

The African held the assault rifle Walters had checked him out on. Aiming high over Bolan's head, he cut loose with a steady stream of full-auto cover fire that shook his entire body.

Morrison reached the trees and fell to the ground, panting. Bolan followed, dropping the woman next to him, then turning to grab Walters and jerk him to cover. Ukewere continued to fire until his magazine ran dry, then fumbled with a full box, trying to remember how to get it into the weapon.

As Walters and the man with the goatee fell to the forest floor behind him, the Executioner dropped to one knee, steadied his elbow on the side of a tree and squeezed the trigger of his rifle.

The two Hutus in the lead fell to the ground in the center of the valley, the bullets shredding their torsos. The rest of the rebels fell back quickly, dropping to the ground or behind available cover.

Bolan took a head count as things quieted. There were roughly twenty Hutu rebels left. He turned and saw that Walters had lifted the blindfolds from the Belgian man and the woman, and cut the ropes that bound the hands of all three. Ukewere had finally forced a new magazine into his rifle, and stood waiting to see what the Executioner had in mind.

"Tater," Bolan said, "you remember the way back to the vehicles?"

Walters nodded.

"Then you and Sal take these three and get started."

The white-haired merc frowned. "What about you?"

"I'll hold them off, make them think we're still here, until you get a good head start. Then I'll follow." Bolan paused. "Now get going."

Walters helped the woman to her feet, and Bolan got his first good look at her. In her midforties, she was still enormously attractive and exhibited an almost aristocratic dignity, even under the present circumstances. She looked vaguely familiar, and the Executioner guessed he had to have seen her onscreen.

Ukewere was suddenly standing in front of him. "I'll stay with you," he said.

Bolan glanced at Morrison. Except for the nasty gash on his forehead, the actor looked to be in fairly good shape. He'd already taken the woman's arm from Walters and it looked like he planned to help her along the way.

Turning to the little man with the goatee, Bolan saw that although terrified, he hadn't been harmed and would be able to run of his own accord.

The Executioner turned back to Ukewere. "Suit yourself," he said. "Switch your selector to semi-auto. The rest of you take off."

Bolan turned to Ukewere. "Don't waste any ammunition. If you see a shot, take it. But the main thing we want to do is to keep them pinned down, remind them that we're still here and they'll get shot if they stand up."

Ukewere nodded.

Bolan and the African waited silently as the footsteps of the others faded behind them. A minute went by, then five. Finally a head rose from behind a cluster of rocks in the middle of the valley.

The Executioner let loose a volley.

Five minutes became ten. Bolan continued to wait, watching the valley with the trained eyes of the sniper. He knew that traveling through the thick forest would be slow going for inexperienced woodsmen, but by now he guessed the others would be several hundred yards away.

Another head peeked over a tree stump.

Bolan fired again, his hurried round striking the stump an inch below his target. The head jerked back out of sight as Ukewere sent two rapid rounds after it.

Out of the corner of his eye the Executioner could see his companion smile with satisfaction.

"We'll give them another five, lay down a few rounds, then take off," Bolan whispered. "You ready to run?"

Ukewere nodded.

The Hutu rebels had decided to play their own waiting game. Ten minutes later, no one else had risked peering from behind cover. Bolan turned to Ukewere, said, "Get ready," then fired a short burst of rounds across the open space.

A moment later the Executioner and Ukewere were racing through the trees after Walters and the others.

10

By the time Bolan and Ukewere caught up with the rest
of the group, they had passed the remains of Big Billy
Rukanwe's underground house and were almost to the
side road where they'd left the Lincoln. After the last
shots had been fired, it hadn't taken the Hutu rebels
long to realize their quarry was escaping through the
woods, and for the past half hour Bolan had listened
to the running footsteps behind them grow ever nearer.

Introductions had come as the Executioner packed
Walters, Ukewere, Morrison, LeFevre and Streak into
the vehicle and slid behind the wheel. As he pulled the
Lincoln from under the brush that had hidden it, the
first of the Hutus had appeared a hundred yards behind them. The vehicle had sped away with rebel bullets falling inches short of the back bumper.

The performers were in high spirits as the Executioner guided the vehicle back along the road toward
Cyangugu. Morrison, LeFevre and Streak had escaped death, and they were ready to celebrate with
laughter, cheers and tears.

"I hate to break the news to you," Walters said over
the merriment, "but we're not out of the woods yet.
Literally or figuratively."

The revelry died a quick death.

Bolan took up the briefing. "By now the Tutsis will have found their dead, and Duke and Bradfordson. They'll put two and two together and head for the plantation. We've got to go get Waseme and Janet. As soon as we've got them, we've all got to get out of the country. The closest border is Zaire."

"If they've found the bodies along the road, they'll have that border sealed up tight," Walters commented.

The Executioner guided the Lincoln toward the plantation. "You're right, Tater. We can't cross at Bukavu," he said. "So we're going across Lake Kivu."

A stunned silence met Bolan's ears.

The plantation appeared ahead. "Sal," Bolan said, "you told me you had relatives in Zaire."

The man nodded. "My uncles and their families."

"Any way you can get word to them?"

Ukewere moved forward, resting his arms on the back of the seat and sticking his head over the top. "They live in the mountains with the tribe," he said, "but I have a cousin who has moved into Goma." He shrugged. "He has a phone. I could try. Why?"

"Because we need them to pick us up on the other side of the lake. And we'll need a place to hide out. There's no guarantee that the Tutsis or the Hutus are going to pay any attention to international boundaries if we're spotted."

The Executioner slowed, then twisted the wheel, guiding the Lincoln onto the road to the plantation. When he stopped in front of the house, both Waseme

Duke and Janet Nyungwe waited on the porch, suitcases at their sides.

"Sal, get inside and make your call," Bolan ordered.

Ukewere got out and sprinted past the women on the porch as they lifted their luggage and hurried to the Lincoln. Waseme bent down, looking through the window at Walters. "He is dead," she said softly.

Walters nodded.

Waseme closed her eyes as the merc opened the door for her, then helped her into the crowded backseat. Janet got into the front between Bolan and Morrison, with LeFevre taking a place on the cowboy's lap.

"I knew I would have to flee when this was over," Waseme said. She looked at Walters. In her eyes Bolan saw a confused mixture of sorrow for the loss of her husband and the excitement of a new life made possible by the same loss. "I just didn't know for sure who I'd be fleeing with."

Twenty minutes later Ukewere rushed out of the house and squeezed into the backseat. "I got him!" he said excitedly. "And my uncle was visiting. He's on his way to alert the tribe right now."

Bolan threw the car into drive. Gravel spun from beneath the rear tires as they hurried toward Lake Kivu.

THE SMALL HARBOR north of Cyangugu was hardly a showplace of the yachting world.

On the other hand, it had boats. A few, at least.

The Executioner braced himself against the rocks overlooking Lake Kivu and peered through the minibinoculars. To the northwest the large body of water stretched over the horizon. A fingerlike peninsula supporting short hills hid the other end of the lake. In between, small vessels in dire need of repair were tied to rotting wooden posts. Trash had gathered along the quayside, and several holes were obvious in the dock.

There was no sign of Tutsis, Hutus or any other human presence.

The binoculars moved along the row of boats. Bolan considered, then rejected each craft in turn. Some were too small. Others bore such obvious signs of disrepair he was surprised they hadn't sunk there in the slips.

The binoculars finally rested on a Carver, roughly thirty-six feet in length. The vessel sported an aft cabin and enough deck space for the entire party—if no one exhaled. The Executioner moved the lenses slowly along the starboard side of the craft to the engine. It was a Kohler, and he saw no signs of rust or other damage.

Bolan lowered the binoculars from his eyes and stared at the boat. It would do, and at least from a distance it looked to be in shape.

Turning, the Executioner hurried back along the rocks to the small plateau where he'd left Walters in charge of the others. He found Ukewere and the aging mercenary standing guard, with the others pressed into semiconcealment behind an outcrop at the foot of the hills.

"I've found a boat and I'm going down to try to get it started," Bolan stated. "Move everybody down to the rocks but keep them out of sight until you hear the engine turn over.''

Walters nodded and began readying the others while Bolan returned to the rocks. The assault rifle slung over his shoulder, he made his way swiftly down a steep slope to the marina, then jogged across the decomposing planks that led to the Carver.

The Executioner's eyes scanned the area as he boarded the craft: quiet, deserted, easy.

Too quiet and too deserted and too easy. It made no sense. There had been more than adequate time for the Tutsi government troops to discover the bodies of Duke, Bradfordson and their own men. They had been lucky to beat the soldiers to the plantation, but by now there should be guards posted not only at the border near Bukavu but at all obvious points of disembarkation.

The Executioner had chosen this marina because common sense told him that wartime and pleasure yachting didn't go hand in hand. Further reasoning told him the Tutsis would know this, too, and therefore the guard would be lighter. Common sense, however, didn't say there would be no guard at all.

Bolan knelt next to the engine, inspecting it. Clean and oiled, it showed no signs of the obvious disrepair that he'd seen on the other engines through the binoculars. Looking up toward the rocks, he saw that Walters had the others gathered at the edge, ready to hurry down the slope.

Again the Executioner's eyes swept up and down the bank. The uneasiness in his soul intensified—the same feeling he'd had in the forest just before he smelled the cigarette smoke of the Tutsi sentry.

The Executioner turned back to the engine. The real test of the Carver's seaworthiness would be in the actual operation. With a deep breath, he cranked it over.

The Kohler coughed twice, started to stall, then began to roar like some giant jungle cat.

Bolan moved behind the wheel as Walters led the way down the slope. He waited, each second that ticked away seeming like an hour as he watched the group move toward the dock.

Behind them, on the small plateau from which they'd come, the Executioner saw a buffalo walk slowly from the trees and gaze down at the peaceful water. The huge creature sniffed the air, then suddenly moved back into hiding.

Bolan dropped to the deck instinctively as the blast of full-auto fire drilled through the cabin window. He had set down the assault rifle to inspect the engine, and drew the big .44 Magnum revolver. More rounds exploded from the other side of the craft as he dragged himself to the port side and peered over the rail to see a Tutsi soldier standing on the deck of a twenty-eight-foot Sea Ray docked two slips down.

The Executioner fired once. The soldier dropped as blood spurted from the cavity where his left eye had once been. Bolan switched his attention to the people still on the dock and saw that all but Walters and Ukewere had dived to the ground. The two men stood blasting away at a Viking Sport Fish on the other side of the Carver.

More gunfire drove Bolan back below the rail. He began to crawl across the deck to the starboard side.

What had happened was painfully clear. Three Tutsis *had* been guarding the marina. They had seen him approach on his recon mission but held their fire, waiting out of sight on the boats until the others came down the slope.

Rising above the rail again, the Executioner saw that Walters or Ukewere had taken out one of the soldiers. The other crouched low on the Viking, still firing his rifle.

Bolan let the red front ramp sight of the Model 629 fall on a point halfway between the man's armpit and waist, then pulled the trigger.

The big .44 Magnum spit flame as it exited the four-inch barrel, then drilled through the Tutsi's ribs and dropped him out of sight on the Viking's deck.

Bolan rose to his feet. "Come on!" he shouted, and watched Walters and Ukewere jerk the others to their feet. "Tater! Pick up a couple of extra rifles and all the magazines you can round up!"

The Executioner hurried back to the wheel as Morrison helped Streak and the women on board the Carver and Ukewere and Walters went after the munitions. Less than thirty seconds later the two men leaped on board.

Without a word the Executioner threw the engine in reverse, backed out of the slip and started out into the lake.

The Carver had barely left the marina when the Tutsi patrol boat roared around the fingerlike peninsula into view.

THE FIRST RIFLE ROUND from the patrol boat fell a hundred yards short as the Executioner kicked the Carver into high gear. Three more rounds followed, then the firing fell off.

But the Tutsi patrol boat didn't slow. The government troops weren't giving up their pursuit; they were just waiting until they got into better range.

Bolan turned to the men and women crowded onto the small craft. He needed someone who could pilot the boat if he was going to be free to lead the return fire. He glanced at Walters, who was jamming some of the newly acquired magazines into the waistband of his jeans. No, the white-haired merc was too valuable as a shooter. And Ukewere had now proved he could pull the trigger, as well.

Droplets of water shot up over the front of the Carver as the craft cut its way through the gentle waves. Bolan's eyes moved to Dusty Morrison, who sat with LeFevre, crowded in between the other two women. Morrison could guide the boat, but he might be able to shoot, too. Somewhere in the back of his mind he remembered that the Western actor was an avid trapshooter and hunter.

"Morrison!" the Executioner shouted over the roar of the engine and the breaking water. "Can you shoot?"

Morrison turned to look at him, then glanced at the assault rifle in Ukewere's fists. "Never shot anything like that before except with blanks in it," he yelled back.

"Streak!" Bolan yelled. "Get in here!"

The little man with the goatee looked up from where he was squatting on the deck, then rose to his feet and stumbled into the cabin.

"Ever piloted before?"

The man shook his head.

Bolan placed his hands on the wheel. "Just like driving a car," he said. "Almost. Just follow the shoreline north. I'll be back before you have to change course."

"But—"

"Streak," the Executioner said, placing both hands on the man's shoulders and looking into his eyes, "just do it."

Streak nodded.

The Tutsi patrol boat had closed the distance considerably by the time Bolan got back on deck outside the cabin. Another shot rang out, falling less than twenty yards behind the Carver's stern. The Executioner ordered the women inside with Streak.

Shoving one of the extra rifles into Morrison's hands, Bolan said, "You know firearms, Dusty, and if you've fired full-auto with blanks, you've fired full-auto. There'll be a little more recoil, but that's about the only difference. Find a place along the rail and keep your head low. The show's about to begin."

The Executioner turned to see that Walters and Ukewere had dropped to their knees behind the rail. Ukewere was practicing with the sights, rising and falling with the waves. Walters looked like the old warrior that he was, a modern-day gladiator in the dressing room beneath the Coliseum waiting for his match to begin.

The Executioner raised the binoculars again and stared through the lenses at the oncoming patrol boat. He was surprised to see that the men on the deck were dressed in Hutu robes rather than Tutsi army uniforms. He handed the binoculars to Walters.

"Well, I'll be damned," the white-haired merc said. "Hutus. I'd lay some money there's some dead Tutsi troopers somewhere in their wake."

Bolan nodded. "That doesn't mean much to us, though."

As if to prove his point, another shot rang out, falling less than a foot behind the Carver.

"Open up," Bolan ordered as he worked the bolt on his FAL to chamber a round.

Suddenly bullets were flying both ways across the lake. The Executioner sighted in on the chest of the nearest man, timed the rising and falling of the Carver as it sped through the water and pulled the trigger.

The colorful robe fell back to the deck.

More rounds were exchanged, but the two craft were still barely within range of each other. The distance, combined with the bouncing waves, brought no further hits.

"Hold your fire," the Executioner ordered.

A moment later the rounds from the patrol boat died, as well. The vessel cut speed until it was riding along the waves like some giant bobbing fishing float. Then it turned and headed back in the direction from which it had come.

"What the hell's going on?" Walters said.

"They weren't expecting resistance," Bolan told him. "They're rebels, not soldiers. They like to kill

Belgians, but their first priority is to take out the Tutsi government." He turned to the cabin and relieved Streak at the wheel, peering through the cracked and broken windows to see that they were passing Kibuye on the east. A few miles to the west he could see the island of Katana in the middle of the lake.

Walters moved into the cabin next to the Executioner. The white-haired merc was grinning. "Let's hope everybody we run into shows an equal lack of dedication to the task."

Bolan started to answer, then stopped as two specks suddenly appeared on the water to the east. He lifted the binoculars to his eyes. "That would be nice, Tater," he said, "but I wouldn't count on it."

"Huh?"

"Those are more Tutsi patrol boats bearing down on us from shore," he said.

THIS TIME the Tutsi patrol boats were manned by Tutsis. As they drew closer, the Executioner could see the camouflage fatigues he'd grown to know during the rescue mission. And as he stared through the minibinoculars, he could see another distinction between the new boats and the one that had given up the chase a few moments earlier.

Both of the vessels racing to cut them off before they left Rwandan waters had M-60 machine guns mounted on the foredecks.

The Executioner gunned the engine, coaxing every ounce of power out of the Carver as they cut on through the waves. Ahead, he could see the northern end of Katana Island in the center of the lake. To their rear, the faster patrol craft gained steadily.

Soon, Bolan knew, they would be within range of the M-60. The American-made machine guns could cut a boat like the Carver to shreds long before their own assault rifles did any noticeable damage to the enemy.

Cutting the wheel, the Executioner guided the Carver along Katana's short northern coast. Ukewere's uncles had agreed to meet them in a small cove approximately nine miles south of Goma. The Zaire Twa would be waiting when the Carver arrived.

But *would* it arrive? the Executioner wondered. He glanced aft again. The patrol boats were nearing the range of their M-60s. The Carver would soon be in Zairian territory, but what if the Rwandans ignored the international boundaries and swept into the cove after them? The Executioner might well bring death to Ukewere's family and its tribe, as well as Walters, Morrison and the others.

The Executioner faced front again. It was too late now to second-guess his strategy. He had made the best decisions he could with the available information, and he had no choice but to stick with them.

It was simple, really. They'd make it. Or they wouldn't.

"Streak!" the Executioner called.

The man hurried into the cabin.

"Take the wheel again. Keep it on course. When we near the cove, I'll send Ukewere to guide you in."

The goateed man visually gulped, then nodded and took the wheel.

Bolan hurried back on deck. "Waseme," he said, "take the women inside and help Streak. The rest of you, get ready. We're about to rock and roll one more time."

From across the water in the Carver's wake, a loudspeaker came on with a screech. "This is the army of the Republic of Rwanda!" a deep voice said in French. "Cut your engines and prepare to be boarded immediately."

Bolan turned to his companions. "You guys ready?"

To a man, they nodded.

"Repeat!" boomed the voice over the loudspeaker. "Cut your engines! Prepare to be boarded! This is your last warning!"

Bolan glanced toward the island. Something caught his eye as he looked away, and he turned back. In the distance he saw another small marina, and just leaving the dock was a small private craft.

The binoculars returned to his eyes. The boat was a thirty-six-foot speedboat, but he couldn't make out the men on deck.

The first burst of gunfire came from the M-60 on the right. Most of the rounds hit the water on the port side of the Carver, but two struck the rail, gouging steel shrapnel from the side of the craft.

The voice boomed again, giving them one final chance.

Bolan's answer was a steady stream of fire that took out two fatigue-clad men on the deck of the Tutsi patrol boat.

Both M-60s opened up, forcing the men on the Carver to the deck. Ragged holes appeared in the hull, but the boat moved on through the water. Bolan, Walters, Ukewere and Morrison took turns, darting up over the rail to return fire, then falling back out of sight when the M-60s erupted.

Bolan raised his head high enough to see around the cabin to the water in front of the boat. The coastline of Zaire was now visible in the distance. "Sal!" he yelled. "Get inside and show Streak the way!"

Ukewere rolled across the deck, came up on his hands and knees and crawled into the cabin.

Bolan waited until the machine guns had quieted, then rose and shot another burst their way. He dropped down again as soon as the big guns returned fire, waiting for the impact of the heavy 7.62 mm rounds on the hull. It didn't happen.

More gunfire exploded behind them, and with it came the distinctive sound of FN FAL assault rifles. But again the Carver sustained no hits. Bolan rose again and saw that the speedboat he'd seen leaving the island was bearing down on the Tutsi boats. Men in the colorful robes of the Hutu crouched on deck, rifles dancing in their hands.

The patrol boats had turned toward the speedboat, their M-60s firing round after round at the rebel craft.

Bolan took advantage of the lull in the battle to rise and hurry into the cabin. He found Streak and Waseme copiloting the vessel, with LeFevre and Janet sitting cross-legged on the deck. Ukewere stood next to the wheel, pointing toward the entrance to a small lagoon on the Zairian shore, now less than two miles away.

The Executioner returned to the deck and raised the binoculars. At least a mile separated the Carver from the patrol boats, but as he watched, the M-60s quieted. He shifted the lenses slightly. The speedboat's deck was littered with corpses, and as he watched, the ruptured vessel sank below the waterline and the bodies floated off into the lake.

The Tutsi patrol boats turned back toward the Carver.

"Collier! We're going down!"

Bolan dropped the binoculars and looked at Walters. The aging merc stood next to the rail, ankle deep in water. The vessel had taken too many hits and was swiftly dropping in the water.

Across the peaceful waves, the Tutsi boats raced toward them.

The Executioner turned back toward the cove where the Twa tribesmen would be waiting. They had closed to less than a half mile now, and the Carver still chugged through the water. But the added weight of the water had slowed the craft to a crawl.

The simple fact was, there was no way they were going to make it.

Bolan's eyes moved from Walters to Morrison. The cowboy knew what was happening, but his face showed no fear. Turning to look back in the cabin, he saw Ukewere standing to one side of the wheel.

Walters, Morrison, Ukewere—good men, all three of them. If it was time for the Executioner to die, he would go in brave company.

Since the beginning of his one-man war against injustice, the Executioner had known he was living on borrowed time. He had dealt death to the world's wicked on an almost daily basis, always wondering when his own time would come.

This day, he might have the answer to that question. But just as he had refused to veer from the strategy he had planned for this escape from Rwanda, he wouldn't deviate from the overall design of his long career against evil. If the next few moments were to be his last, he would make the most of them. He would go down still fighting the fight he had fought for so long.

And a few more Tutsi soldier-terrorists would go down around him.

Bolan's jaw set as he brought his rifle to his shoulder and waited for the oncoming enemy. Walters suddenly pointed to the rear of the Executioner, then shouted, "Collier! Look!"

The water had risen to knee depth as Bolan turned to see the Twa tribesmen launch two canoes from the Zairian coast. A pair of men jumped into each of the hide-covered boats, and the long, slender vessels began bounding over the gentle waves.

The warrior looked over his shoulder to see the Tutsi boats a quarter mile away. Through the binoculars, he could see the M-60s rotating toward them.

"Tater! Morrison!" the Executioner shouted. "Get the others ready!" He stuck his head in the cabin. "Sal! You pilot until they've come alongside!"

The aging merc and the actor sloshed through the thigh-high water into the cabin, returning a moment later with Streak, LeFevre, Waseme and Janet. They waited at the starboard rail as the canoes paddled forward.

Bolan hurried to the stern, dropping to his knees in the cool water. The top of the hull rode less than an inch above the waterline as he raised the assault rifle and sighted in on the patrol boats.

Behind him, the Executioner heard the excited voices of the Twa as the canoes bumped the Carver's hull. He glanced over his shoulder to see Morrison and Walters pushing Streak and the women over the sides of the boat, then turned back, sighted down the barrel of the assault rifle and pulled the trigger.

Rounds ripped from the weapon in a steady stream. One cammie-clad Tutsi fell to the deck of the patrol boat to the Executioner's right. Bolan swung the rifle to the side, hosing the boat to the left. Two more of the Tutsi soldiers went down. The magazine cycled dry and the bolt locked open as Lake Kivu finally climbed over the side of the vessel.

Bolan found himself treading water as the boat disappeared through the water beneath him. Dropping the empty rifle, he turned and swam toward the nearer canoe. A man who looked like an older version of Salewe Ukewere dropped his paddle and reached out, grabbing his arms and helping him into the craft.

As he drew the big .44 Magnum revolver from wet leather, the Executioner saw Morrison, LeFevre and Waseme in the canoe between the Twa. Morrison had retained his rifle, and fired a steady stream of 7.62 mm NATO rounds at the closing Tutsis.

Bolan turned as the Twa paddled madly for shore. In the corner of his eye, he caught a glimpse of Janet in the other canoe. She was flanked by Walters and Ukewere, who were firing steadily at the patrol boats.

The M-60s opened up again, drilling into the water around the canoes as the Twa paddled in choreographed unison. They were forty yards from the lagoon now, but the Tutsis were almost on them. Bolan squeezed the handgun's trigger repeatedly until the hammer fell on an empty chamber. He pulled a speedloader from his pocket and swung the cylinder from the frame.

The other three men continued to lay down fire as the Executioner jammed a fresh load into the big revolver. The M-60s roared on, their giant steel bullets splashing the water inches from the canoes. One round skimmed past the Executioner's knee, slashing through the hide at the top of the primitive boat.

Then, seeming louder than the explosions from the patrol boats, Bolan heard Walters's rifle bolt click open, empty. A split second later Ukewere's did the same, followed by Morrison's.

As the Executioner slammed the cylinder back into the Smith, he saw Walters drop his rifle and draw the twin .45s.

Then, suddenly, rifle rounds entered the foray again. But they lacked the familiar ring of the FALs, instead sounding like AK-47s on full auto.

Bolan fired two more rounds at the Tutsis, then turned to see two Zairian patrol boats shooting forward through the water from the south. Uniformed men stood on deck, their Kalashnikovs vibrating as they blazed away at the invading Rwandan craft.

New explosions boomed just to the north of the canoes, and the Executioner did an about-face to see a third Zairian vessel heading their way, a 12.7 mm machine gun on the deck of the craft firing on the Rwandan boats.

A final volley of 7.62 mm rounds drilled into the canoes. Bolan heard a muffled grunt a second before he emptied the rest of the .44's cylinder at the Rwandan boats. As the Magnum roars died in his ears, a low moan drifted across the water.

Then the Rwandan craft began a hasty retreat, the Zairian patrol boats close at their heels.

Bolan turned toward the other canoe as the Twa guided them into the lagoon. Walters had dropped his .45s and now held Sal Ukewere's head in his lap.

A huge hole gaped in the center of Ukewere's chest, blood covering the man from feet to throat. His eyes stared blindly at the sun.

On the shore, Bolan saw dozens of men holding spears, bows and blowguns. They jumped up and down in excitement as the canoes neared.

With the machine guns and rifles still roaring in the distance, Tater Walters reached down and closed Sal Ukewere's eyes.

In January, look for Gold Eagle's newest
anti-terrorist weapon

MICHAEL KASNER

BLACK OPS

UNDERCOVER WAR

America's newest strike force, the Black Ops commandos operate
beyond the reach of politics and red tape. No rules, no regulations,
just results. Objective: retribution against U.S.-directed terrorism.

Don't miss UNDERCOVER WAR, the team's first Black Ops
mission: to save Cuba's fledgling democracy from Communist
hard-liners and the Mafia.

Look for it in January, wherever Gold Eagle books are sold.